A WOLF IN MY BEDROOM

by
T.K. Wade

I0592859

INGRAMSPARK EDITION

*****

PUBLISHED BY:
T.K. Wade on IngramSpark

Cover Art Illustrated by:
Chris Buffaloe

*****

A WOLF IN MY BEDROOM

*****

Table of Contents

Chapter 1 – Eyes in the Dark

Samantha Peri lay next to her husband Lucas. It was nearing midnight, and the only sounds heard about the house were the light rumblings of thunder and the sounds of a crying child. Lucas was occupying himself with a novel. He really wanted to just go to sleep, but his wife was having some difficulties doing that.

"She's only eight months old, Lucas," she said in a whimper.

Lucas turned a page and replied without looking at her, "Too old to be crying like this. She needs to figure this out."

Samantha tittered for a little bit. Soon, she said, "But there's a storm coming."

"*We're* not crying about it, are we?" replied Lucas.

"But she's *eight months*."

Lucas looked at his wife. He had a very strong gaze, and it had always caused the woman to swoon when she looked into his eyes. He said, "All the better, don't you think?"

The child's cries still pierced the air into their room. It was constant, and Samantha was having trouble hearing it. Several times, she started to leave the bed, but a strong hand from Lucas would change her mind. The thunder clashed louder, and the sound of rain pattering on the roof now added to the crying of their daughter.

The woman remained restless but still for a time listening to it all. She suddenly turned to her husband and said, "I think I may have left her window cracked."

"I doubt it," he said.

"No, I am serious. I was sitting here thinking about it. The wind could get in… or a burglar."

Lucas Peri shook his head. "Dear, I seem to remember last time you ran to save your daughter it was a loose screw in her crib."

"It *was* really loose," she explained. "You saw it. I had to tighten it."

"Half a turn," he said. "It was hardly about to collapse with her in it."

"Maybe, if she jostled it enough——."

"No," interrupted the husband with a calm yet stern voice.

Samantha patted her lap with both hands as she tried very hard to think of something else. In reality, she knew he was right. Little Darlene needed to learn that it was fine to sleep alone once in a while. The truth was that she and Lucas might not always be there for her–even in storms such as this.

Samantha also saw it from another perspective. Darlene–their daughter–was still quite accustomed to having her parents run in there to comfort her. Teaching her to settle for less was–in effect–breaking her heart. She would–for the first time in her life–realize that she could not always depend on someone to help her. This was, perhaps, what upset the mother so much. As another clash

6

of thunder rolled over the house, she yearned all the more to run out to sate the child's fears for just one more night.

Little Darlene could not help but cry. She was alone, and there was a lot of scary things in her room that she did not understand. The lights were off too which only made them worse. The storm brought with it terrible sounds and sudden flashes. The room would briefly light up and cast uncanny shadows about the bedroom making it a very terrible and unfamiliar place. This is why she cried. Crying was a way to fix the problems in her short life. The very act brought in two people whom seemed to make these terrible things go away, and until now, it had worked well.

A gust of wind hit the window on the far side of the room. Darlene peeked up from where she lay in the crib. The window was rattling on the outside. It was a hanging window that could be propped open when it was a nice, sunny day, but at nights–especially stormy ones–it was usually locked shut. That was not the case on this night. The wind was making it rattle and strike against the sill as if begging to be locked down. Darlene continued to cry.

There was a flash of light. Darlene saw two yellow eyes watching her from through the window. She stopped making noise. What was it? Was it a monster? She stared attentively at the darkened window to see if she could make it out again. For a while, all was silence, and then suddenly, there was another flash of lighting. She saw those same eyes again, but they were now inside the room. Still, she watched. The creature was in there with her… somewhere. What was it? Should she cry again?

The wolf had chosen his house well. The foolish human had left the window unlatched. He would have an easy opportunity to rid them of their child. It would be an easy kill–a simple bite to the neck. It would be easy enough to take away and eat.

Slowly, the creature walked towards the unprotected crib. She had seen him, but what good would that do? She could not fight back. She could not shoot her with a gun. She was powerless. All little human girls were powerless, and soon, she would be his.

He looked though the bars of the crib and saw her stare at the window with wide, fearful eyes. He enjoyed it for a moment. It was that oblivious look that human's had when they knew something was wrong but had no idea what it was… or where it might come from. Satisfied, he leapt up into the crib and began his growl.

The child turned around and looked into his cold and terrible eyes as he bared his teeth and let his saliva flow onto the cloth in front of her. He snapped a few times to make her tremble while he drew ever closer to the little thing. But here, the girl did something unexpected. When he was only an inch away from her, she placed her little hands on his nose… and just held them there.

The wolf ceased all movement. He looked into her eyes, and she into his. She did not seem as afraid as he thought she would be. It was more of a wonder in some respects. Perhaps, she was too young to be afraid, but then… why had she been crying earlier? Here was the monster right in front of her, yet she seemed rather pleased just to hold onto his nose as if to say, "Hello there."

The wolf backed away from her touch. Somehow, he still felt it. What an odd sensation it was. She just looked at him with those little eyes like he was some sort of stuffed animal. He shook his head and leapt back to the floor. His meal would have to wait... until later. Even as he walked to the window, the girl continued to look at him with some sort of silly fascination. He would need time to sort this out. When the wolf was gone from the room, Darlene lay down and went right to sleep.

"She stopped crying," said Samantha.

"It's for the best," said Lucas turning off the lamp. "At least now, we can go to sleep."

The mother continued to sit there a bit longer. With sadness, she muttered, "We broke her heart."

Chapter 2 – Preschool

Darlene was five years old. She had been going to Busy Bee Preschool for a couple of years, and she really had grown into it. The little girl had red hair that was tied up into pigtails. She never really liked having them tied up, but her mother thought it was cute.

Today, she was laying out on the ground during recess with her friend Cindy. They were coloring in books while all the other children were playing on swings and slides. Darlene had only met Cindy a month prior, but they really got along well and usually tried to stay close to one another while at Busy Bee.

"His name is Ozzy," said Cindy while she tried to stay in the lines. "He's a dragon."

"What color is he?" asked Darlene who likewise was concentrating on her art.

"Pink polka dot," came the reply. "The other color is just green like it should be."

"Can dragons have polka dots?" asked Darlene.

"Why can't they?"

Darlene tried to explain, "I never saw an animal that had polka dots."

Cindy shook her head. "Dragons aren't animals. They're people. They can be polka dotted if they wanna be."

Darlene looked at her friend incredulously. "Aren't I people?"

"Sure, you are."

"One time, I wanted to have brown hair, but my hair stayed red. I don't think being people means you can choose what you look like."

"But you're not a dragon," explained Cindy.

"Oh, I didn't think of that," said Darlene. "Whoops. I wish I was a dragon now."

"Dragons can't have red hair," added Cindy.

"Why not?"

"Dragon's don't have *any* hair."

It was all making a lot of sense to Darlene. Cindy was probably the leading expert on dragons in Busy Bee Preschool. She felt like she was learning a lot about the strange creature, and if she was to ever meet one, she would know a thing or two about them. However, Darlene was unsure if she would ever actually meet one with the daily routine that had been set up for her. Dragons did not often fit into a little girl's life. Cindy must have just been special or something.

"What about you?" asked Cindy as she flipped to another page. She had given up on the previous one–too many mistakes.

Darlene did not take long to answer, "His name is Shadow."

"What kind of creature is he?" asked Cindy.

"He's a wolf."

"Just a wolf?"

The redhead did not understand what Cindy meant by that comment. She said, "Wolves can be people too, but I don't think they can be polka dot."

"What color is he?"

"Dark gray. You can't even see him when the lights are out."

"Not even a little?" asked Cindy with newfound curiosity.

Darlene thought about it. "Well, sometimes you can see his eyes. They're yellowy."

"Does he talk to you?"

"Sometimes," replied Darlene. "He usually just sits there and looks at me."

"What do you do when he does that?"

"I look back at him. He doesn't care."

"It sounds a little boring," thought Cindy aloud. She really had not intended to be rude, but Darlene did not like hearing it too much.

"What do you do with your dragon?" asked Darlene in a snippy way.

"He tells me about different ways he's going to eat my brother, and I give him ideas which he likes more than his ideas."

Darlene remembered meeting Cindy's brother. He really *was* annoying. She asked, "How many ways can a dragon eat your brother anyways?"

"Lots," was the only reply to her question. "Do you and Shadow talk about things?"

"He talks to me about whatever I want to talk about. He doesn't like to talk about himself. I usually just talk about you, and my mommy, and daddy, but I don't have a brother he could eat."

Cindy said, "My mommy told me a story where a wolf was mean to three pigs and blew down their houses for no reason. I think wolves are mean."

"I'll ask him if he did that," said Darlene.

"Let me know what he tells you then, but I wouldn't be friends with a wolf anyways. If one wolf is bad, then maybe, they're all bad."

"I don't think Shadow is bad," said Darlene with a frown.

Cindy explained, "I'd like him more if he was pink polka dots."

Darlene did not want to discuss it further. She felt like she was just going to get her feelings hurt. She decided to talk about other things until they were allowed to go home. Maybe then, she could find out if the story Cindy had heard was true.

Chapter 3 – A Question of Pigs

Darlene had been quiet at the dinner table. Her father, Lucas, had noticed the silence and had been keeping an eye on the girl. Her mother, Samantha, thought to try and see if anything was bothering her. "Darlene, did you have a good time at preschool today?"

The redhead was pushing around the peas and carrots on her plate–trying to mix them up into her mashed potatoes. It was the only way she could enjoy the meal. "It was neat," she said while working her food around.

"Well… what was neat about it?" added the mother.

"About what?" the girl asked looking up.

Lucas placed his silverware down on his plate a bit noisily and said, "Your mother was asking about your day at preschool."

"She was?" Darlene was suddenly paying attention, and it was obvious.

Samantha somehow found it funny and giggled. She asked, "Is there something on your mind?"

"Yes," said Darlene resolutely. "I am worried about Shadow."

Lucas released a sigh of frustration and went back to focusing on his food. Samantha gave him a look before returning to her daughter. "What are you worried about?"

"Cindy told me about this wolf that was really mean to three pigs. He destroyed their homes for no good reason.

I am worried that it might have been Shadow… or some other wolf he knows."

Samantha nodded with apparent interest. "I heard about that story too."

"Oh, then it *must* be true!" said the girl rather vexed at the revelation.

"Have you asked Shadow about it yet? Maybe, it wasn't him. So far, Shadow doesn't sound so bad."

Darlene shook her head. "Not yet. I was going to ask him tonight. Only… I am afraid he will get annoyed with me for bringing it up."

Lucas suddenly broke in, "I'll ask him for you. I've been wanting to meet him anyways." Samantha gave her husband a scolding glance… of which he entirely ignored.

Darlene, once again, shook her head. "I told you: he only wants to come to me when I'm alone. Every time either of you come by, he's always gone. I try to make him stay, but he won't."

"I'm sure he is just shy," said Samantha.

Darlene nodded profusely at her mother's comment. "He is *super* shy."

Lucas seemed a little irritated. He wiped his mouth after finishing his food and said to his wife, "Seems a little rude of him to be spending so much time in our house without at least paying me rent."

"*Honey*," was all Samantha said. She really just wanted him to drop it, and he did. In fact, he left the table entirely to go wash his plate in the sink.

The mother returned her attention to Darlene and said, "I'm glad you made a friend, dear, even if he doesn't want to see us."

The little girl replied, "I like Shadow a lot. I'm sorry he keeps hiding like that."

"Well, did you want to finish up your plate and go and meet with him again?"

"He won't come out till you're all asleep."

Samantha nodded. "You need sleep too, honey."

"I know," said Darlene going back to eating.

Later that night, Samantha lay in bed with Lucas. For a while they did not talk. Lucas read a novel and Samantha was looking at a magazine. Eventually, the wife said to him, "I *like* that she has an imaginary friend. There's nothing wrong with it, and I don't care what you think. So there."

Lucas looked at his wife who had gone back to her magazine as if she had said nothing at all. The little fuss she had just made actually amused him. It was even the tiniest bit cute. The husband smiled a little and looked back at his book, yet he was not reading it. He said to her, "Is that your way of telling me that you have your *own* imaginary friend?"

"Oh, he isn't imaginary," she claimed–turning a page.

He nodded and replied, "Should I be jealous?"

"*Very*," she said proudly.

"Is he a wolf too?"

"No, he's a tiger."

Lucas snorted a little. "A tiger, huh? How is he in the sack?"

Samantha was shocked as she looked at him, but then she smiled and said, "You should know already." Lucas grinned and tossed his novel away. The tiger was about to pounce!

Little Darlene waited in her room with the lights off. She listened carefully for any sounds that were out of the ordinary. In a whisper, she said, "Shadow? Shadow, are you there?" No reply.

She squirmed and snuggled more into her blankets. Turning her head, she watched the hanging window. It was only slightly open. Suddenly, she saw it move a little. The girl listened very carefully and thought she heard little taps on the floor. "Shadow?" she quietly called. Still, there was no reply.

After waiting a little while longer, Darlene reached over to her nightstand and flipped on her lamp. When she turned back, she was face to face with the large menacing eyes of a wolf that was standing right over her.

Chapter 4 – Shadow

Darlene looked into the wolf's eyes in silence. The wolf likewise gazed back with intensity. There was a certain aggression to it–a desire left unsated–for this wolf remained unmoving as he stood above the girl. If he wanted to, he could have her, but he resisted the urge and simply chose to look at her.

The five-year-old allowed him to do this. It had not been the first time; although, it had not been a nightly event. Although she never understood it, she felt as if this creature was trying to see something–something inside of her. As giving as she wanted to be, he was always left disappointed. He would soon shake his head and turn away with frustration.

"Are you mad at me, Shadow?" asked Darlene once she felt it was safe to talk.

The wolf spoke in a deep and growly sort of manner, yet it was somehow softened by the girl's very presence. "You have never angered me, Darlene." Shadow sat at the foot of her bed and purposefully looked away from her.

"Why do you look at me like that sometimes?" asked the girl.

The reply, "Why do you look back?"

"Daddy told me that it's polite to look people in the eyes when they look into mine. I was only trying to be polite."

The wolf snorted lightly and replied, "You must do what you think is best. I shall do likewise. Again, I tell you that you have not angered me."

"Thank you, Shadow," she said respectfully. He did not react to this in any notable way. She went on to say, "May I ask you a question that… may make you mad anyways?"

Shadow peered over at the girl. Darlene took this to mean what he was fine with it. She continued, "Today at preschool, Cindy told me that there is a story about a wolf who blew down the houses of three pigs. Have you heard of it?"

Shadow appeared to consider it. He soon remarked, "I am not certain what you mean by 'blew.'"

Darlene explained, "With his breath. He blew down their houses to get at the pigs. Can wolves do such a thing?"

Once again, the wolf snorted. "I know of no wolves with such abilities; although, I cannot speak for all wolves. Nevertheless, I have little respect for a wolf that must rely on such an ability. A pig is easy prey for a wolf, and he should need little than his wits to slay one of them."

Darlene was really attempting to think through Shadow's strange way of speaking. She was getting better at it with practice, and much of what he said made sense to her. "I thought he only wanted to destroy their homes. Would a wolf kill a pig?"

Shadow chuckled for a small time without answering. He found the question of this girl to be rather amusing. "You are so young," he said with an amused air.

"I'm five," replied Darlene.

"Five years could be an eternity for a pig, and even then, they can grow quite fat and useless as they age. They lack any manner of wits to contend with the dangers of life. Even if they were to develop such pluck as to build a house for their own protection, their innate imperfections would spoil the plan, and I would inevitably still find my way inside."

He went on as he stepped towards the listening redhead, "Sloth and gluttony breeds lapses in sight. Pigs are too easily compelled to such temptations, thusly, a door remains unlocked, a window remains unlatched, or they simply trust that they are above such things as predators such as I." He once more glared closely at the girl and said, "Where I am no fool in such things, in contrast. My eyes, ears, and mouth are always open, and those who are not looking my way will find themselves betwixt my jaws awaiting the next moment to be crushed and swallowed." He ended his speech by showing his toothy maw dripping with saliva and awaited the girl's reaction.

Darlene patted her lap a couple of times and asked, "So, you really would eat them?"

"Does that frighten you, Darlene?"

"I'm not a pig," was the reply.

Shadow's aggressive moment passed swiftly after hearing that. He sat down on his haunches and snorted again. "Indeed, you are not a pig."

Darlene shook her head and said, "I don't think pigs would ever live in houses anyways. All the wolves would have eaten them up before they got a chance to build them."

"I agree with you," said Shadow. "Your friend's idea of a wolf seem reliant on an embellished view of a pig. A wolf has no need to blow down the walls of any house, and if a pig were to build one at all, it would be made of nothing more than its slop of which it would consume for fear that it would be stolen by another. They are stupid, and my kind shall have no trouble at all with liberating your world of them."

Darlene nodded as if she understood; although, much of what he said was a little fuzzy in her mind. She then asked, "So, did talking about the pigs make you mad?"

"I am not angered by you, Darlene," he simply said.

She added, "Are you mad at Cindy for telling me that story?"

"I do not know her," said Shadow dismissively.

"You seem a little mad though," said Darlene shrinking down under her sheets. She was getting very sleepy.

Shadow cocked his head as he looked at her for a bit. "I am not angered by you, Darlene," he repeated.

The little redhead yawned and sleepily asked, "If I was a pig, would you eat me up?"

"Yes," said the wolf without much thought.

"Well," she said with another yawn, "at least, it would be you and not some monster." Darlene closed her eyes.

Shadow remained quiet and watched the girl fall into slumber. It was a rather therapeutic activity to watch an innocent, little human child slip into the unproductive trance which every living creature must succumb to at some point. It was marvelous to observe it happening in action. Here, she was nothing but a meal for him, and he could consume her at his leisure; however, he remained still and only watched.

When he was satisfied, Shadow slowly and carefully crawled down onto the floor. With his teeth, he yanked the lamp's cord from the wall so that the room was once again bathed in darkness. The wolf left Darlene alone for the rest of the night.

Chapter 5 – Cold

It was the next morning. Samantha had prepared breakfast for her husband and daughter; however, Darlene had not showed up at the table as she usually was known to do. Lucas had managed to keep her in the routine pretty regularly, so it was odd to not see her on time. The husband noticed the absence as well and asked, "Did you forget to set her alarm, dear?"

Samantha thought about it. Without answering him, she made her way to Darlene's bedroom door and knocked. "Darlene, you'll miss breakfast if you don't get up." The mother heard the girl mumble something indistinctly, so she decided to just go on in.

The room was dark with the drapes pulled. It appeared that Darlene was still asleep–or at the very least, uninterested in getting up presently. "Darlene, really," scolded Samantha. She walked over and switched on the child's lamp, but it did not come on. Confused, the mother got down and noticed that the cord had been pulled out, and there was something wet and viscous on it. "What happened to your lamp, honey?" Darlene just grumbled again.

Samantha replaced the cord and flipped on the lamp. It was here when she noticed something was wrong with her daughter. "Honey, you look so pale." She felt Darlene's forehead and noticed that it was very warm.

Darlene opened her eyes and looked up at her mother. "Mommy," she whined, "I don't feel good."

"You're definitely sick, honey. No preschool for you today. I need to take your temperature and decide if you need a doctor or not."

"But I gotta tell Cindy about the pigs."

"Not today," said Samantha resolutely. "Don't even think about leaving that bed." But then she noticed something. She walked over to the window and checked behind the curtains. "Oh, honey, you need to keep the window shut at night." She pulled it closed.

"But Shadow can't get in if I do that," said Darlene with a cough.

"Not another word about Shadow. I'll be back in a moment. Do you think you can eat, honey?"

"I'm not hungry," she said.

"Then I'll being you some orange juice," Samantha said as she left the room.

"Well?" asked Lucas who had just finished his breakfast.

"Our little girl is ill. She feels like she has a fever too. I have to call Busy Bee and let them know she won't be showing up today."

Lucas nodded looking plenty concerned. He stood up and said, "It's probably just a cold, but it wouldn't hurt to call her doctor just to be sure."

"I'll do it," she said. "Just let me handle this, dear."

He half chuckled and said, "Well, she *is* your daughter."

Samantha was dialing the phone as she said, "She left her window open all night to let Shadow in. I just knew that that would be a problem on one of those chillier nights."

Lucas huffed and went silent while his wife explained the situation to the preschool. Shadow was a touchy subject presently, and he decided not to air his objections just then. When his wife was through with the call, he said to her, "You know, dear, we might as well call it quits with Busy Bee anyways. She's been there long enough."

The mother began pouring orange juice into a cup. She replied, "She likes it there, Lucas. She just met Cindy and everything. I just don't think it is a good idea to separate them right now."

Lucas left for a moment to get the thermometer. He placed it on the table and said, "She's ready for Kindergarten, and I'm going to make the arrangements today, dear. She can still be friends with Cindy, and I even think it would be a good idea for her to visit us once in a while."

Samantha felt a little cornered being that she was more worried about Darlene at the moment, but she nodded and said, "All right. Go ahead. I'll take care of Darlene today." And so she left to do just that. Samantha was not upset with Lucas; she was upset that her little girl was growing up, and that was all. She knew he was right—even if he could have been a little more tactful about it.

Darlene's temperature had only been one hundred degrees, and the doctor said that it was a mild cold. He explained that children were more prone to fevers with colds and had prescribed her some medicine to help with the symptoms. All in all, it was not such a bad thing to happen.

Later in the day, Cindy showed up at the house with her own mother and wanted to see her best friend. Samantha warned her not to get too close since she could get sick too, and the little girl agreed to be careful.

"Darlene, are you awake?" asked Cindy when she entered the room.

Darlene slowly sat up and tried her best to not look sick. "Careful, I've got a cold."

"I'm sorry," said the visitor. "We all made a drawing for you. Do you want to see it?"

Darlene nodded, so Cindy held up a large picture drawn with crayons. It was all the children from Busy Bee, but she was able to pick out Cindy and herself in the picture because of the dragon and wolf next to them. "What do you think?" asked Cindy.

"It's great. I love it," said Darlene with her weak voice. "Can you leave it here?"

"Sure. I hope you get better soon."

"Thank you," said Darlene–coughing a few times. "Before you go, I wanted to tell you that I talked to Shadow about the pigs."

"What did he say?" asked Cindy curiously.

"He said he wouldn't need to blow down the house. He said he would just sneak in and eat them. I believe him too."

Cindy shuffled a little bit before replying, "Well, if you ask me, I think Shadow is a bad wolf if he wants to eat innocent piggies."

Darlene frowned and almost said nothing at all, but soon, she was compelled to say, "The pigs probably deserved it if the wolf ate them."

Cindy did not feel like fighting with Darlene while she was sick. She vehemently disagreed with what she heard, and she really just wanted to leave so that her friend could get better. "I'll ask Ozzy the dragon if he knows any dragon cures for colds, okay?"

"Thank you," said Darlene laying back down. "Thanks for coming."

"Your welcome," replied Cindy politely, and then she left the room.

Darlene was annoyed with Cindy for calling Shadow a bad wolf. How was he bad? He was her best friend. The little girl decided that Cindy may know a lot about dragons, but she knew nothing of wolves. If she could not say nicer things about Shadow, then perhaps, they should not even be friends. That was what she had decided.

Chapter 6 – Disgust

Darlene had slept a lot throughout the day. She only ate a little food and turned the rest of it away. Samantha was quite worried about her daughter despite hearing that it was normal. That night, the mother sat with her daughter and asked, "Are you sure you don't want to eat just a little more? Maybe, a peanut butter and jelly sandwich?"

Darlene shook her head. "I feel like I just want to go back to sleep again. Maybe, tomorrow."

Samantha felt Darlene's head. "It feels like your fever has gone down. The medicine must be working."

The girl coughed. "But my throat still feels bad."

"It will go away in a few days, honey. Are you sure you don't want anything else to eat?"

Darlene shook her head again. "No, mommy. But can you tell daddy something?"

"What is it?"

"Tell him I am fine with kindergarten. I think me and Cindy can't be friends anymore after she said mean things about Shadow. I never said mean things about Ozzy, so it wasn't fair."

The mother ran her hand through Darlene's red hair. "I'll tell him, but you really should reconsider. Cindy seems like such a nice girl."

"I don't care," whined Darlene with a cough. "Although, it was nice of her to visit me and bring me that picture." She looked at this very picture and seemed to be reconsidering where she stood on the matter.

Samantha noticed it too and said, "It is a *very* nice picture that she brought you. Is that Shadow next to you?"

"Yes. He looks a little different though. I want to show it to him, but he can't get in tonight if you don't open the window, mommy."

Samantha placed her hand to her daughter's chest and said, "No. Shadow stays outside tonight. Good night, dear."

"Good night, mommy," said Darlene turning onto her side. Samantha turned off the lamp and left the room, leaving the door open a crack.

Darlene was so ill that she just went directly to sleep; however, sometime during the night, she awoke to the sounds of scratching at the window. She could see two yellow eyes looking at her from outside and knew who it was. With a lot of aches, the little girl got out of bed. She first went to close her bedroom door, and then she went to the window and pushed it open. No sooner than she did this did she get back into bed which is really where she wanted to be. "Hi, Shadow," she said with a cough.

The wolf stood in the darkness of her room with only his yellow eyes visible to the girl. She heard him speak, "What is wrong with your voice?"

"I'm sick," she said miserably.

Shadow growled for a moment. Darlene sensed that he was annoyed or something; she was not sure. "I'm leaving," he said.

However, Darlene turned on her lamp and said, "Wait, don't go."

Shadow was at the window. He stopped at her request, but he did not look very happy about it. He momentarily turned to look at the sickly girl staring down at him, and the sight only made him cringe and look, once more, away.

"What's the matter, Shadow? I don't think I have a wolf disease. It's just a human cold. Wolves can't get colds. I had my mommy ask the doctor, and he said so."

Shadow said nothing at first, but he really did seem aggravated. That same aggravation was present when he replied, "I do not care about your illness, and right now, I care little about you."

The words made Darlene's eyes automatically filled with tears. She rubbed them away with her arm saying, "You don't mean that. Why would you say that?"

The wolf turned back to the little girl and snapped, "Well, just look at you! Pale and sickly flesh! Disease! What is that to me?!"

"Don't yell at me!" she coughed and lay back down to her pillow where she openly wept and coughed. She was just too ill to fight with him, even if it was the first time this had happened.

Shadow snorted and turned back to the window so that he could leave; however, he stopped when Darlene weakly cried out into her pillow, "Why are you treating me like this, Shadow? I love you."

Shadow remained still and quiet. It was obvious that he wanted to leave, but he chose to stay. Even so, he was only tolerating the girl. At present, there was nothing he really liked about her. She was a whimpering pile of diseased meat. It was disgusting.

Darlene thought the wolf had abandoned her while she still whimpered into her pillow, but when she finally looked up, he was sitting upon her floor looking at her with frustration. "You're staying?" she asked.

"Yes," he replied shortly. "But I may not come tomorrow. When do you expect to be relieved of your illness?"

"My mommy said it could go on for a few days."

The wolf only snorted and said nothing else. Darlene added, "Cindy came by, and I told her about the pigs. I told her that they probably deserved to be eaten by a wolf."

"They all deserve it," said Shadow.

"She called you a bad wolf, and I defended you. You're not a bad wolf... are you?"

"I can only be who I am," he said. "I don't enjoy being questioned on such grounds. Neither you nor your friend have any right to decide such things. I am a wolf, and I lead a wolf's life. What others think about right and wrong–good and evil–mean nothing to me or any other wolf."

Darlene was rattled by his speech. "Please, don't hate me, Shadow. I really love you." The wolf remained silent and simply continued to stare.

The sick girl tried to change the topic. "Well, anyways, she brought me that picture from preschool. You're in it, if you want to see it."

Shadow saw the picture and decided to go have a look at it. He sat in front of the poster board with the crayon artwork on it. All the people were stick figures, and they were all standing on a green hill with mountains in the background. He noticed the dragon for a moment but could not really figure out what it was. Finally, he saw himself. He said aloud, "Is this scribbly thing supposed to represent me?"

"It doesn't look anything like you," she said. "But nobody at preschool has met you, so they did their best."

Shadow cocked his head to the side still looking at it. After a long pause, the wolf said, "It is an acceptable representation considering the ignorance of your friends. I approve."

Darlene smiled. "You do? You like it?"

The wolf turned about and said, "Yes, and now, I am leaving. Goodbye." He made his way to the window.

"You're coming back, right?" asked Darlene hopefully.

"In a week. When I return, I shall make sure this never happens again."

"How?" the girl asked curiously.

"Leave that to me," he said moments before he was gone. Darlene got up one more time to pull the window shut and reopen her bedroom door. She went back to bed wondering what Shadow meant. Was he able to prevent her from getting sick?

Chapter 7 – A Mother's Confusion, A Daughter's Honesty

Later on in the week, Darlene was feeling much better. She still had a cough that refused to go away, but even that was lessening hour-by-hour. She had visited her kindergarten class to have a look around and meet some of the kids there, and she felt as if it would not be too bad; however, the first day for her had not yet happened.

On one evening, Samantha sat with her daughter simply to chat. "I haven't heard you talk about Shadow lately," said the mother. "Has he not been visiting you with the window closed?"

Darlene sighed and seemed to be a little upset. "I'm sorry, mommy, but I had to let him in just once."

"Did you open the window, Darlene?" asked the mother accusingly.

"Only for long enough to let him in and back out. Also, I only saw him once… but… he wasn't happy to see me."

Samantha's curiosity was instantly provoked. She had never heard something like this before. "He wasn't?" she asked. "Why was he upset?"

"Because I was sick. He didn't even want to talk to me. I think he stayed because I started crying, but he still left a little later."

Samantha was rather unsure what to say to this. It was one thing to have an imaginary friend, but it made little sense for such a thing to turn on you just because you're sick. The mother thought very hard about what it could mean while at the same time trying to convince her girl that Shadow probably was just in a bad mood. Shortly after leaving her daughter, she confronted her husband.

"I think Darlene is upset that you were not there for her enough while she was sick," she said to him.

Lucas was instantly flabbergasted. "Dear, you know I love you with all of my heart, but sometimes, the things you say are ridiculous."

"Lucas, I'm serious!"

The husband rolled his eyes. "Was it not you who told me that I was to stay away from her on days like this? Why am I being punished for doing as you wished? I would have been happy to spend time with her, but you would have had a hissy fit about it, and don't you dare deny it."

Samantha huffed and replied, "I'm not denying it, Lucas. I'm just saying that this is the problem we are having right now. Who cares why it happened? She was telling me that Shadow was mad at her for being sick. She said he did not even want to be around her. But if you think about it, that may have been you all along."

Lucas joked, "I thought I was a tiger, not a wolf."

Samantha gave him a weak hit to the chest and urged, "You need to go in there and talk to her! Let her know that you still love her!"

He grabbed her arm to stop her; although, it was not because she was hurting him. He said to her, "I'll be happy to if you'll let me, dear. Besides, I agree with you. It sounds like she is just upset about that thing I *didn't* do that *wasn't* my fault."

"Just go in there," she ordered.

Lucas chuckled and let her go. As he walked away, he remarked, "Why aren't you this feisty every night?" She rolled her eyes and said nothing.

Lucas caught his daughter sitting by the window as if waiting for someone. He looked at the scene for a moment before coming in saying, "Hey, honey. Waiting for Shadow?"

Darlene was startled but smiled when she saw who it was. "Daddy! I don't see you in here very often." She whispered, "You know this is a girl's room, right?"

"Yes," he replied. "It's full of all sorts of icky things." He sat on her bed and patted next to him. Darlene took the hint and sat up next to her father. After putting an arm around her, he asked, "Are you feeling better?"

"Much better, daddy," she said with a nod.

"I'm very happy to hear that. You do know that I dearly want you to be happy and well, right?"

The little girl nodded. "Yes. I know you love me, daddy."

"That's good," he said giving her red hair a tousle. "You know that I would never be mad at you for being sick, right?"

"I know," said Darlene.

Lucas asked curiously, "Did you think I was mad?"

"No, never," she said firmly. "That was Shadow. He was not happy with me at all when he saw I was sick, but you don't have to worry because I think he knows a way to make me not get sick anymore."

The father was momentarily confused. "But I thought... Honey, don't you think that Shadow's reaction happened because I wasn't around much for you while you were sick?"

The question baffled the girl more than anything she had heard in a while. She finally said, "I don't know what you mean. You're not Shadow. He's a wolf. He was the one mad at me."

Lucas tossed out an idea, "Were *you* mad at yourself for being sick?"

"Only because it upset Shadow," was the reply. "I love him."

Lucas' frustration boiled up to the surface. He turned the girl towards him and said, "Now, honey, this whole Shadow thing is going a bit too far. You and I both know that he isn't real."

It was as if the words had made no sense to Darlene. She only replied, "What?"

Suddenly, the bedroom door was nearly kicked open. Samantha snapped, "Lucas, can I talk to you–like right now?"

"Can it wait? I'm spending time with my daughter."

"No, it can't. She needs to sleep anyways. Goodnight, Darlene. Daddy's gotta sleep too."

"I understand," said Darlene a bit mystified by all the odd behavior of her parents.

Lucas grumped for a moment and then kissed his daughter on the forehead. "Goodnight, honey."

"Goodnight, daddy," she said; although, she was not really that sleepy. It was still early yet. Nevertheless, her father was dragged out of the room. She went back to the window to watch for Shadow in case he came back early.

In the hallway, Lucas had to stare down his wife who was glaring back at him. The man was entirely flustered with her, and it was taking some effort not to start yelling. "You are impossible," he said outright. "Didn't I do what you wanted?"

She pressed a finger to his chest and accused, "You were about to destroy her dreams! What's next–Santa Clause?"

"This whole Shadow thing is getting out of control," he countered. "She's not living in reality. Heck, she said that the blasted wolf has a way to make her never get sick again."

"She's just a child," said Samantha. "She'll grow out of it. Seriously, Lucas, what you almost did was completely insensitive!"

Lucas glared at her shaking his head. "This conversation is over. The tiger needs a nap." And he turned to walk to the bedroom. Samantha followed him there and was not ready to give up her side of the argument. Either way, they never could convince the other of anything, and so the night ended with frustration.

Chapter 8 – A Touch on the Nose

It was a night before Darlene would go to kindergarten for the first time. She still had not made up with Cindy, but she was thinking about doing it soon. Her mother had really been pressing her about it, and the picture in her room was a constant reminder that it was likely the right thing to do. After all, the longer Darlene had been away from her, the more she missed her friend.

Although, kindergarten and the Cindy situation was presently on her mind, it was Shadow that was keeping her awake. It had been exactly one week since she last saw the wolf. She had put the window open so that he would have no trouble getting in this time. The girl wondered if he really could make her never get sick again. He had never lied to her before.

It was already pretty late. She sighed thinking maybe he was not going to show up after all. She had been watching the window pretty regularly, but she never did see anything. Maybe, he was still mad at her. Maybe, he was gone forever. The thought genuinely upset the girl. She whimpered out in a whisper, "I didn't mean to get sick."

Darlene suddenly felt a hot breath upon her left ear, and then a growling voice replied, "Do you think I even care?"

"Shadow!" she cried.

"Go back to sleep," he replied, but Darlene switched on her lamp. He was in bed with her. His yellow eyes stared harshly at the girl. He was angry, and she could tell. "What did I tell you to do?!" he asked in a growl.

"I can't sleep now! You came back to me. Please, tell me you aren't still mad. I'm not sick anymore. I don't even have a cough."

Shadow placed a paw to her chest. His claws were out, and it hurt a little. "Lay back down, child. I am in no mood to play around."

Darlene slid back down under the sheets as he kept his claw to her chest. She winced from the pain, but she never seemed all that frightened. The girl said to him, "You told me you were going to take care of my getting-sick problem. Is that what you are doing?"

"Yes," said the wolf. "Do you remember when we first met?"

"No," she replied. "It's been forever."

"Listen clearly to me, girl, that you shall know whom you have made a companion of. Near the time if your birth, I snuck into this very room. You were still sleeping in a crib, and you had been left alone by your parents. Do you know what I came here to do, Darlene?" He applied pressure with his claw. The nails were close to piercing her skin.

Darlene winced but replied, "I don't know. I can't remember that far back."

Shadow appeared to grin with his toothy maw. "I came here to kill you. I was going to tear up your flesh and devour it." Darlene's eyes widened, but she said nothing. The wolf continued, "You were weak and defenseless. There was nothing you could do to stop me. I was going to sink my teeth into your little neck and taste of your blood.

Do you understand, Darlene?" His other claw joined the first on her chest. She only nodded in silence.

The wolf bared his teeth and lowered his head to her face. In a nasty voice, he said, "To this very day, I have wanted to do that to you, Darlene. In fact, I'm thinking about it right now. If I were to kill you right now, would you even be able to stop me?"

Darlene said nothing. The wolf snapped, "Would you?!" He growled loudly getting closer and closer to her face; however, Darlene suddenly held up her right hand and pressed it to his nose.

It was as if Shadow lost every ounce of his bark the second she did that. The growling stopped, the claws retracted, and his eyes opened wide in shock. The girl began rubbing his nose slowly trying to sooth him, but the wolf yanked himself away from her. "How... How did you know?!"

"How did I know what, Shadow?" she asked.

He barked, "What you did that night! Why did you do that?!"

"I love you, Shadow," said Darlene.

"But I was going to kill you!"

"But you didn't."

"But I was going to!"

"But... you didn't," the girl repeated.

The wolf moved over top of her again and said, "But I still want to."

She rubbed his nose again which made him shutter with anger. She said, "I understand, Shadow. You're a wolf. But we're friends now, right?"

Shadow released a long groan of displeasure. He was definitely angry, but he was also diminished. He hated himself in that moment. The wolf had told her the truth, and it had meant nothing! So... he replied in the only way he could think, "Very well."

Darlene smiled putting her hand down. Shadow looked into her eyes and said, "Darlene, I need to know that you are mine. I need to know that you will be mine from now until the end. If you cannot agree to this, then I will leave you forever. Do you understand?!"

"I'm yours, Shadow," she said without much thought; although, Shadow could see that she meant it. "I love you," the girl added.

"Count to five," he ordered.

"Why?" the girl asked.

"Just do it," said Shadow.

The girl looked at the wolf curiously and then began counting. "One... two... three... four... fi—"

Darlene gasped as she suddenly began to inhale out of control. Shadow exhaled, and it was as if his breath was flowing into her lungs by force. Although, she was surprised by it, she allowed it to happen, and in a moment, it was over. She panted looking up at him wondering what had happened.

Shadow was quiet for a time as he stared down at her. Soon, he asked her, "Darlene, do you feel me inside of you?"

Once more, she placed her hand on his nose. Shadow yelped and snapped at the air around the girl before running to the end of her bed in a temper. Darlene giggled and said, "Why do you hate when I touch your nose?!"

"Don't talk to me!" he snapped.

The girl got from under the covers and gave the wolf a hug from behind. He let her. He hated it with all of his heart, but he let her. "I love you, Shadow," she said amidst her embrace.

Shadow started to fight against the hug for a little bit, but soon, he just fell down to his side with the girl on top of him. He felt like a wounded animal. It was miserable to be treated this way, yet he allowed it as he had on the first day they had met.

After yawning a few times, Darlene crawled back under her covers. "I'm so glad you came back, Shadow. Will you stay here for a while before you leave?"

"Yes," said Shadow remaining at the foot of the bed.

"Am I ever going to be sick again, Shadow?" she asked closing her eyes.

The wolf snorted and then sighed. He soon replied, "You shall never know disease again in your life, Darlene."

"Thank you," she said and drifted off to sleep. Shadow rested on his side for most of the night. When the light of day began to break into the room, he pushed himself up with a groan and made his way out.

Chapter 9 – The Book

Darlene was six years old, and it was her birthday. All her friends from kindergarten were there–especially Cindy. They were best friends, after all. There was cake and ice cream for everybody, but of course, the real treat for the girl was the stack of presents waiting for her in the corner of the living room. Even though Darlene was chatting with her friends, she kept glancing over at them wondering what was going to be inside.

"Ozzie couldn't come," said Cindy. "Dragon's don't come to birthdays because dragons don't have birthdays."

"They don't?" asked Darlene. "Why not?"

"Ozzie was never born," explained Cindy as if she understood it perfectly. "Dragons just show up one day and try to be friends with people."

"That makes sense," said Darlene with a smile.

A nearby girl named Rosy said, "Dragon's don't exist, and if one did, it couldn't talk. You're making it up."

Cindy shook her head. "My dragon is real. Darlene knows a wolf, and he talks to her all the time."

Darlene nodded and explained, "That's right. His name is Shadow, and he is my friend even though he'd rather eat me."

Rosy usually had a comeback for everything, but Darlene's reply only produced a gaping stare out of her.

Cindy was a bit shocked to hear this as well. It was her who said, "Shadow wants to eat you?"

Darlene looked at her best friend and realized her mistake. "Oh! Don't worry, Cindy. He won't because he's my friend. Friends don't eat one another."

Rosy said, "That sounds creepy."

"How come?" asked Darlene. "Did I not explain it right?"

Samantha came in just at that moment. "Is everyone having fun?!" All the children cheered creating a very ear-piercing sound. Darlene added, "It was the best ice cream ever!"

Cindy added, "It was really very nice, Mrs. Peri."

Lucas walked in quietly and leaned against the doorframe. He was not really interested in participating in a girl's birthday party, but it was somehow pleasant to watch from a distance. He also enjoyed seeing his daughter happy.

Samantha moved suspiciously to the table of presents and looked knowingly at her daughter. Darlene gasped and shouted, "Is it time?!" With a smile, the mother motioned for her to come over. "It's time!" screamed Darlene. Everyone came over to the table to see what she was going to get.

"Which one should I open first?" asked the birthday girl.

"Mine!" cried out Cindy picking it off of the table.

"It's only fair because you're my best friend," said Darlene as she took it.

"Mine next," urged Rosy.

Darlene opened the present and was happy to find a pair of friendship bracelets with both of their names on each one. She did not even say anything; she simply hugged Cindy. They had had a few rough moments in the past, and this was a wonderful gesture. "I know what these are!" said Darlene. "We talked about doing something like this."

Cindy replied, "Yes, we did. Now, we can stay friends no matter how we disagree." They put on their bracelets and hugged one more time. Rosy thought it was all kind of silly. It was not like the cool pony movie that she got for her.

Darlene liked all of the presents that she got from her friends. Some of them, she was not really sure about. She was not much of a fan of ponies, but she promised she would watch it anyways. Soon, all the children had to go home, and Darlene saw them all off to their cars as their parents came to pick them up. When she came back inside, the girl saw her mother holding one last present.

"Who did I miss?" asked Darlene. "I thought I opened them all up."

The mother replied, "This is from me to you, dear."

"Oh! Thank you, mommy!"

Lucas was still there watching the whole thing. He wanted to see what Samantha had bought for her. He was curious why the present was so very small. What could it be?

Darlene sat down at the coffee table with her mother sitting next to her. She tore open the paper and found a little book inside. She was having trouble reading the title, but she saw a picture of a wolf on the front that caught her attention. This wolf was very similar looking to Shadow.

"What is it?" she asked her mother.

"It's called *Little Red Riding-Hood*. It has a wolf in it–a big bad wolf. I know how much you love your friend Shadow, and I thought you would enjoy hearing me read this to you."

Darlene stared at the cover for a little longer and then suddenly embraced her mother. "Thank you, mommy! I would love that!" Samantha hugged her daughter, but when she looked up at her husband, he was scowling at her.

Before Darlene had gone to bed, Samantha met with Lucas alone in their room. He was not in a good mood, and she knew why. Even so, she asked him, "Why were you looking at me like that? It was her birthday."

Lucas crossed his arms and replied, "That book—"

"What about it?" she interrupted. "She likes wolves. This is a book about a wolf."

He released a frustrated sigh and shook his head. "The whole Shadow situation is already out of control. I just think she needs to break the habit as soon as she can. It won't help with you feeding her mania with a book like that."

"A mania?!" she nearly shouted in surprise. "Is that what you think she has? Are you her shrink now?"

"No, but if this goes on for another year, I wouldn't be opposed to sending her to one."

"Not a chance," said Samantha. "Our daughter is perfectly fine. Besides, this is a story about a bad wolf. Maybe, she will change her mind about Shadow after this. Did you think about that?"

"Well, I—"

"No, you didn't," she broke him off again. "Maybe, that was my plan all along. While you were thinking about sending our daughter to the crazy farm, I was applying a more practical solution to the problem."

Lucas was not at all diminished by her jockeying. In fact, he even smiled at her cute attempt to shut him down. Slowly, he walked up to her staring deeply into her eyes. She became uncomfortable. She did not know what he was doing. Why was he not getting annoyed?

Lucas took hold of her arms and leaned in to kiss her on the lips. She swooned and kissed him back. Afterwards, he said to her, "Thank you."

Coming back to reality, she squirmed out of his grip and said, "I'm going to read the story to her now."

"Go ahead," said Lucas.

"You might as well just wait for me tonight."

"I *shall* wait for you."

"It might take a while," she added.

"I hope she enjoys it."

Completely flustered, Samantha marched away from her husband. She only momentarily stopped to look back. He was still standing there grinning like an animal at her. She almost smiled back, but she had to force herself not to. A moment later, and she was gone.

Chapter 10 – Little Red Riding-Hood

"Once upon a time," read Samantha to her daughter, "there was a little girl who was very pretty and adored by her mother and grandmother. Her grandmother likely adored her even more, for it was her who sewed together a red riding-hood for her to wear, and for this reason, the girl was always called Little Red Riding-Hood."

"What is a riding-hood for?" asked Darlene.

Samantha guessed, "I think it is something you wear when you ride on a carriage, dear."

"Oh," said Darlene and then nodded for her mother to continue.

"One day, Little Red Riding-Hood's mother gave her daughter a bun and some butter and said, 'Go and take these to your grandmother, for I have heard that she isn't well.' And so, the girl agreed to this and set out down a path into the woods which lead to another village where her grandmother lived."

"Why didn't she *ride* there?" asked Darlene.

Samantha sighed and said, "I suppose the father was out with the buggy or something."

"Oh," said the girl again and then waited to hear more.

"While in the woods, Little Red Riding-Hood met with Master Wolf who wanted dearly to eat up the little one, but as there were woodcutters in the forest, he would not dare. Instead, Master Wolf asked her, 'Where are you going?'"

Darlene suddenly answered, "To grandmother's house."

The mother looked at her daughter suspiciously for a moment, but then she continued the reading, "The poor child who did not know it was dangerous to talk to strangers in the wood replied, 'I am going to see my grandmother who is sick. I am taking her this bun and butter so that she might feel better.'

"'Does she live very far away?' asked Master Wolf.

"'Oh yes,' said Little Red Riding-Hood. 'She lives past the mill that you can see so far away from here, and then she is the first house on the left.'

"'Well then,' replied the wolf, 'I would like to see her too. I shall go by a different path and meet you there. We shall see who gets there first!' And then he ran off without waiting for an answer."

Samantha stopped for a moment to look at her daughter. Darlene was entranced by the story. She had never been so focused in all of her life. "Who got there first?" the girl asked.

"I'll continue," said Samantha looking back at the book. "The wolf did not simply take a different path, but he took every shortcut he knew of to get to the grandmother's house in good time. There, Master Wolf knocked upon the door, *rat-a-tat-tat!*

"'Who is it?' came a reply from inside.

"Master Wolf imitated the little girl's voice and replied, 'It is I, your granddaughter, Little Red Riding-Hood! I brought you a bun and a little pot of butter that my mother has sent.'

"The kind grandmother who was not feeling good, could not tell the difference between Master Wolf and her granddaughter, so she called out, 'Draw the peg back, and the bar will fall.'"

"What?" asked Darlene.

Samantha explained, "It must be how they locked doors back in the old days."

"Oh, okay," said the little girl wanting her mother to continue.

"Master Wolf did as he was told and pulled the peg from the door. When he heard the bar fall, he swiftly pushed open the door, flung himself upon the old woman who was in bed, and ate her up in only a moment–for he had not even a single meal in three days. Quickly, he shut and locked the door again, went to lie down in the grandmother's bed, and waited for Little Red Riding-Hood."

Darlene asked, "How did he eat her up so fast?"

"Well, it said he was *very* hungry, dear," replied the mother.

Darlene did not seem convinced; however, her interest was not at all diminished. Samantha continued, "In a little while, Little Red Riding-Hood did come, and she knocked on the door, *rat-a-tat-tat!*

"'Who is it?' came the voice of Master Wolf.

"Little Red Riding-Hood, hearing the wolf's gruff voice and was frightened at first; however, she believed that it was due to her grandmother's illness. So she answered, 'It is I, your granddaughter, Little Red Riding-Hood! I brought you a bun and a little pot of butter that my mother has sent.'

"Making his voice much softer, Master Wolf replied, 'Draw back the peg, and the bar will fall.'"

Darlene leaned forward with anticipation. It was making her mother a little nervous, but she still continued reading, "Little Red Riding-Hood drew out the peg, and when she heard the bar drop, she entered into the house. When he saw her coming in, Master Wolf hid under the bedsheets so that very little of him was seen. He told her, 'Put the bun and the little pot of butter on the chest, and come get into bed with me.'

"Little Red Riding-Hood undressed and got into bed, where she—."

"What?" asked Darlene confused.

Samantha looked at her daughter. "What is it, dear?"

"Why did she undress?"

The mother read the lines over again to herself. For some reason, she had not really paid attention to it. In fact, she had not remembered that part from her childhood. "I... I don't know. It's a very old story, dear. Maybe, that was simply a custom they had back then."

Darlene was breathing very deeply. She pointed at the book and asked, "What happens next?"

58

Samantha sensed something was wrong; however, she chose to keep reading, "Little Red Riding-Hood undressed and got into bed where she was surprised to see what her grandmother looked like without any clothes on. The little girl said, 'Oh grandmamma, what long arms you have!'

"'All the better to hug you with,' said Master Wolf.

"'Oh grandmamma, what long legs you have!'

"'All the better for running with, my dear,' said Master Wolf.

"'Oh grandmamma, what big ears you have!'

"'All the better to hear you with, my dear,' said Master Wolf.

"'Oh grandmamma, what big eyes you have!'"

Darlene took hold of Samantha's arm as she leaned forward with anticipation. The mother swallowed and continued, "'All the better to see with, my dear,' said Master Wolf.

"'Oh grandmamma, what great big teeth you have!'

"'All the better to *eat you with!*' And as he said these words, the wicked wolf flung himself on top of Little Red Riding-Hood and ate her up."

Darlene suddenly let out a gasp like she had just been through a big ordeal. Samantha flipped through the book in confusion. "I don't understand," the mother said.

"Understand what?" asked Darlene. "That was amazing!"

"The ending," said Samantha upset. "That's not how it ended."

"What do you mean? Wasn't that the ending? He ate her, right?"

"But you don't understand, dear. There was a woodcutter that came and saved them both."

"How?" asked the little girl. "Master Wolf ate them."

The mother explained, "No, a woodcutter comes and finds him asleep and cuts open his belly to let them out."

Darlene shook her head. "No, mommy. That would never happen. They died."

"What?"

"Mommy, they died. The wolf ate them. I know the book didn't say, but when a wolf eats someone, they bite their necks and all the blood goes everywhere. You can't save them from that!"

"Darlene!" cried the mother in shock.

"It's true! Wolves rip people to pieces and eat them until nothing is left. Shadow told me! But Mommy, it's okay! That's just what wolves do! I love the book, mommy! Can I have it?"

Samantha's hand was shaking. She looked at the book and then at her daughter. "Please," asked the girl. "I really loved it. I just want to look at the pictures till I can learn to read it myself."

The mother nervously handed her daughter her birthday present. Darlene held it to her chest with a smile. "This is my favorite story ever. Thank you, mommy."

Samantha kissed her daughter, and with a trembling voice, she replied, "You're welcome, dear."

Lucas was waiting as promised when Samantha got into bed with him. He immediately sensed that something was wrong. "Samantha?" he said to her.

She looked at him as if startled. He asked, "What's the matter?"

Samantha shook her head and replied, "I don't know. I just read it to her and… I just don't know."

Lucas could see that she was about to cry. He took her into an embrace and rocked her a little. "It's okay, honey. Calm down, and we'll talk about it." Samantha held onto him for a while before she could calm down enough to speak again.

Chapter 11 – The Interpretation

When Shadow arrived through Darlene's window that night, he found her looking through a book. At first, he was uninterested, but the girl wanted him to hear about it. "Just look at the pictures," she said as she forced the book in front of his face.

"It looks like a wolf," said Shadow.

"It looks like *you*," she corrected. "Doesn't it?"

Shadow cocked his head to one side as he examined one of the illustrations. He soon said, "Darlene, I find the picture satisfactory. Who is the girl seen with him?"

"That is Little Red Riding-Hood. The wolf eats her."

"Does he?" his interest gained suddenly.

"Yes," nodded the girl with a smile. "My mother just read this to me. I think I can tell it to you… if you like. Since it's a story about a wolf, you might like it."

Shadow seemed more focused than usual. He was more the type to come in just out of habit. He normally despised conversation and storytelling. In this case, the wolf sat down before the girl and looked her directly in the eyes. He said, "You may begin."

Having just heard the story, Darlene recalled it very easily. Even minor details came back to her, and she managed to relay the story in its truest form for the wolf to interpret. And interpret the story, he did. Shadow paid very close attention as Darlene turned the pages showing off the illustrations one by one. As she neared the end, the wolf began to act strangely. The creature began to bare his teeth and breathe a little more harshly.

"And then the wolf ate her up," finished Darlene. "And that is how it ended." Shadow saw a picture of the wolf leaping upon the girl who was mostly covered by blankets. He licked his chops as he stared at the picture for a short while.

Darlene wondered why he would not speak. She asked, "Aren't you going to tell me what you think of it?"

Shadow looked into her eyes once again. He continued to remain silent. Darlene just smiled and went silent as well. He did this sometimes, and she was used to it. Eventually, Shadow spoke, "I suppose you are aware that when a wolf kills, it is a messy affair."

Darlene replied, "I told mommy about that. She said that there was also supposed to be a woodcutter that cuts them out of the wolf's belly at the end."

"No," said the wolf clearly. "That is stupid and does not belong in this story."

"That's how I think too," nodded the girl. "I think that the book just told the story one way–even if it was happening a much more messy way."

"That *is* how it happened, Darlene," said Shadow. Darlene went quiet and listened. The wolf continued, "Let me tell you the truth of this story since you seem to be a little confused.

"If you remember, Little Red Riding-Hood met with… Master Wolf and was not at all afraid of him. The story suggests this was a case of naiveté, but the mother would never have allowed a stupid daughter to walk such grounds unless she trusted the little girl's instincts. No, Little Red had met this wolf before."

"She did?" asked Darlene.

"Shut up," said Shadow, and she obeyed. He continued with his interpretation, "The girl in the story wore red because she meant to tease this wolf. She knew how much he savored the blood of children. Her grandmother had nothing to do with the gift.

"Perhaps, the threat of woodcutters was real, I do not know; however, the wolf chose not to sate his lust presently. Instead, he retaliated against her tease with his own. He proposed a race to her grandmother's house. They bantered about this in a very silly way, but each of them knew the other perfectly. She accepted his terms and betrayed the location of her grandmother's house. This sent something of a thrill through the wolf, for she had in that moment formed a commitment to see the scheme to an end–Mother and Grandmother be damned."

Darlene wanted to speak, but Shadow was starting to look angry. She did not like to upset him further when he got like this. Shadow barked out more of the story, "Little Red Riding-Hood took her bloody time getting to the house. I don't imagine she cared anything for her Grandmother who was about to be slaughtered by Master Wolf. Indeed, once he found a way into the house, he bit deeply into the old woman's neck and tore her to bits, and yes, I am sure he was quite hungry after dealing with that little *harlot* out in the forest.

"He ate as much as he could and likely drug her mangled remains under the bed–which, might I add, was drenched in red. Still, the game must continue, and he took his place under the bedsheets awaiting the arrival of one Little Red Riding-Hood.

"Oh, she came, all right," the wolf said in a growl. "She showed up and acted as stupid as she always did. The games you humans play are inane and worthy of every bite and scratch I can think of, but the wolf was playing by her rules presently. He was doing this because *she provoked it!* It is no wonder that when she entered and clearly saw what had been done upon the bed of her sick Grandmother that she acted as if there was nothing amiss. What did she care? Tell me, Darlene!"

Darlene only responded, "I don't know."

"That's because you're stupid," said Shadow moving closer to her. "Master Wolf asked her to enter into bed with him. At any moment, she could have left, and the wolf would have let her. She was in control. She owned him in those moments, yet she not only did as she was asked, but she disrobed beforehand."

Shadow snapped at the girl causing her to draw back a little. "The gall!" he cried. "She removed the red cap! There was now nothing to see! The very color that had attracted him was gone, and here she was quite close to him in bed. All of her flesh was exposed, and underneath that flesh was blood–*real* blood! One bite, and that blood would flow! But even here, Master Wolf could do nothing but play her wretched game!

"Oh, yes, Little Red Riding-Hood saw him in that moment. She saw everything that made him a wolf, and had the nerve to act surprised. And so the questioning began, and he answered those questions with lust that was nearly boiled over. One after another they came, and with every one, the pink of her skin turned more and more the color of her cap. It was no longer a tease; it was an invitation! She wanted it! She was begging him to kill her whether she knew it or not! Stupid girl! You had it all! You had a life! You have a family who loved you, and you threw it away to a wolf!

"He *tore* into her with much relish! It was a frightful mess! Bones were tossed to the left and right, and I am convinced that there was no recognition left in her corpse once he had completed his act! That's what happened, Darlene! That's what happened to your Little Red Riding-Hood! There's only so much a wolf can take before he will falter and tear into his prey like the beast he is!" And then Shadow went quiet; although, he was growling quite constantly.

Darlene's heart was pounding. Her eyes were very wide as she looked into those of this beast. Neither one of them knew what the other would say or do. It was a very tense moment for both of them; however, the girl suddenly said, "I'm gonna hug you."

"Don't you dare!" he snapped.

Darlene slowly crawled around the wolf as he barked and growled at her. She put her arms around his neck and let herself fall with him in her arms. Shadow yelped and then seemed to calm down. "There, there," she said to him. "I liked your story more."

"I hate you," he wailed.

"I still love you anyways," she said and began to rub his nose. "Please, stay with me tonight."

"I will," he replied, and so he did.

Chapter 12 – No Such Thing

A couple of nights later, Lucas came into Darlene's room. At first, the girl smiled and said, "Hello, daddy!" However, the father did not answer and only closed the door. The girl instantly felt like something was wrong. There was a look in her father's eyes that she did not like.

Lucas picked up a chair and set it in front of his daughter who was sitting on her own bed. Darlene remained quiet and waited to see what this was all about. Lucas faced his daughter sternly for a short time before finally saying, "Dinner will be ready shortly, honey, but we need to have a very important talk first."

"Okay," was all she said.

Lucas went on, "A couple of nights ago, you said things to your mother that really upset her. You talked about what a wolf really does to their victims. You really frightened her, Darlene."

"I did?" asked the girl who was honestly surprised to hear it.

"You did," he said with a nod. "Even though what you said may have been true, it was not the sort of thing a little girl of your age should be dealing with. I assume you learned about it from either a friend or TV. Which is it?"

Darlene shook her head. "Shadow told me."

Lucas raised a stern finger and was, in fact, looking rather angry. Once again, Darlene was surprised. The father said, "I don't want to hear it. I am going to say this here and now so that you entirely understand me: Shadow is not real. He never was real. He is a figment of your imagination, and you need to accept that. Your mother feels the same way now that we've had time to discuss it. I will no longer play these games with you, Darlene."

The little girl was intimidated, and she hated it more than anything because it was her father doing it to her. It felt like betrayal. She felt herself melting down into a mixture of sorrow and anger. In a trembling voice, she said, "That's not true."

"Yes, it is, and I never want to hear you say otherwise. In fact, I want you to admit to me, right now, that Shadow doesn't exist."

"I won't," she protested–nearly in tears.

"Darlene," he said with a pause, "you frightened your mother. This is finally becoming a real problem. If you don't cut out these games right here and now, I'm going to spank you and there'll be no dinner afterwards either. You'll do what I say because I'm your father." Darlene was becoming more and more miserable. She felt like the whole world was falling apart. The father added, "Now… admit to me right this moment that there is no such thing as Shadow… so we can move on."

Darlene scowled for a moment as she tried very hard not to cry. Was this how he had always felt? Did they never believe her? It was like meeting her father for the first time in her life! Shadow was real, and she knew it! But now, she was going to be punished if she told a lie, and she had never, ever lied to her parents before.

Lucas waited for longer than he likely wanted to as he glared into his daughter's eyes. Finally, the girl took a deep breath and said, "Shadow isn't real. I made him up." Lucas nodded, leaned forward, and kissed her. "You're a good girl, sweetie. Get up and come to dinner, all right?"

"Fine," she replied halfheartedly.

Lucas got up and left the room. Darlene was really upset. She hated herself for what she did. When she happen to look at her window, she could see two yellow eyes looking back at her. It was like her heart broke right at that moment.

Darlene made her way into the dining room without saying a word. Samantha was just laying out the food. "Hey, honey," she said with feigned cheerfulness. "Did you have a good talk with your father?"

"I guess," said Darlene.

Lucas kissed his wife and, as if nothing had happened, asked, "What's for dinner, dear?"

"I thought cheeseburgers would be kind of fun. Darlene, you can make them up any way you want." The mother pushed towards her a plate with a bun and a burger paddy on it. There were all sorts of other things on the table that she could add to it. Samantha was really hoping that the meal would mend some things between the two of them. It was hard enough letting Lucas do what he did. The last thing she wanted to be was the "bad guy."

Darlene looked at her plate. She was still upset. It was not fair what her father made her do, and she was blaming her mother as well. Lucas sat down and proceeded to assemble his cheeseburger the way he wanted as if there was no reason to wait. The girl felt ignored. It hurt. Samantha was doing the same, but she kept looking up as if encouraging her daughter to do likewise. Meanwhile, all Darlene could think about was the way Shadow was looking at her.

Darlene took hold of her plate and pulled it closer to her. She looked at it like she was trying to visualize something. Lucas suggested, "Make your burger, sweetie."

The girl said, "I want ketchup."

Samantha picked up the bottle of ketchup and almost gave it to her, but Lucas stayed her hand. He said, "You want ketchup, what?"

"I want ketchup, please," she corrected in an ill tone. The bottle was given to her.

Darlene overturned the plastic bottle and began to squeeze. The red liquid quickly began to squirt out until the burger was entirely covered with it; however, she did not stop. She continued to squeeze, and squeeze, and squeeze! Ketchup was getting all over the plate, and some was even misfiring onto the tablecloth. The more of a mess it made, the more violently the girl squeezed the bottle.

Samantha was frozen by what she was seeing. She had no idea how to react to it. Lucas, on the other hand, struck the table and commanded, "Darlene, you stop that right now!"

In response, Darlene tossed the bottle off to the side where it hit one of the window curtains. Without another moment passing, she dug her fingers into the mass of red and hamburger meat and began sloppily forcing it into her mouth. She growled as she did this and chewed nosily with her mouth wide open. Her face was covered in a mass of red, and in that moment, she looked like some sort of feral animal.

Lucas shot up from the table and swiftly walked around to grab the girl. Darlene saw him coming and lunged up onto the table. Samantha screamed as her daughter dug into her own hamburger in the same way. Lucas reached across the table and grabbed the girl's leg– dragging her back towards him. Darlene kicked, growled, and gnashed her teeth with all the meat and red sputtering this way and that. Samantha could not take any more of it. She stood up and walked out holding her hand to her mouth.

Lucas carted his growling daughter back into her room, placed her down onto his lap, and proceeded to deliver a very firm spanking. Darlene screamed and cried because it hurt. The reality and pain was suddenly real! Her father was really hurting her! But then she, again, saw the eyes of Shadow looking at her from behind her window, and she did not feel so bad about it anymore. She accepted the punishment in total silence. In her mind, the wolf was devouring her, and for some reason, she liked it.

Chapter 13 – Doctor Rule

The room appeared to have a playful atmosphere; however, there was a gloom to it as well. Despite there being a number of board games, toys, and plush animals lying about the room, there was also an office table with a number of papers and pens laying on it. The wall was rather plain with various pictures depicting waterfront properties with docks stretching out behind them. There was also a framed certificate upon the wall for a gentleman named Doctor Thaddeus Rule, Doctorate in Child Psychology.

Doctor Rule was a broad shouldered man. He was brunette with a beard. Proportionally to most other people, he was a very large man in muscle; however, no one ever saw him as scary in the least. He had gentle eyes that always served him well to put others at ease. His eyes were possibly his greatest gift, and this was a fact that he knew and accepted personally.

Presently, Doctor Rule sat in a comfortable chair. His right ankle was resting upon his left knee which formed a makeshift table for a thick notebook in which he often marked up with highlights from his sessions. He always seemed like a remarkably relaxed gentleman in everything he did.

Across from him was a large couch. Darlene sat directly across from the doctor. On her right was Samantha, and on her left was Lucas. Introductions were presently being made. Darlene did not want to be there. She did not want to talk to this man. This whole thing was intended to convince her of a lie, and she did not want to be a part of it.

Her parents were suddenly the enemy, and she would never give in to them.

"Darlene," came the resonant voice of Doctor Rule.

The little girl almost gasped when her name was called. There was a sweetness to it that surprised her. She looked into his eyes, and he smiled. "What?" she replied.

"Darlene, you don't have to talk. It's really up to you. I was just curious about you and Shadow."

"What about him?" she asked. She had inexplicably forgotten that she had planned not to say anything to this man.

Doctor Rule smiled and replied, "Your wolf friend. Your parents tell me how important he is to you."

She crossed her arms. "They made me say he wasn't real."

Lucas interjected, "Because he is not."

"See?!" she shouted.

Doctor Rule nodded and looked up at the two parents. "Could you both please wait outside?"

Lucas and Samantha looked at each other for a moment, and then they nodded and left the girl alone with the strange man. Darlene persisted in looking ill about the whole thing. She scowled and would not look this man in the eyes.

Doctor Rule interlaced his fingers and simply let the girl have time to calm down. He never stopped smiling. Darlene refused to look at him for a time, but soon, she could not help but do it. When she saw him smiling, she sneered and looked away again.

Doctor Rule said, "I am not your enemy, Darlene. I really do want to hear all about Shadow. You don't have to tell me anything, but it would please me if you did. Your parents aren't here to stop you."

Darlene looked at him again. She asked, "Will you believe me?"

The man chuckled. "Well, I haven't heard anything to believe yet. You've been so quiet. Would you like me to ask you questions to help you along?"

She was suddenly interested. "Go ahead."

"What is Shadow like?"

Darlene answered, "He's gloomy most of the time. Wolves are always gloomy. They get... *growly* when their day doesn't go like they want it to. He still talks to me though. I have to usually talk to him first."

"What can make a wolf's day not go so well?" he then asked.

She paused to think about it. "When he doesn't eat. Wolves like to eat."

"What do wolves eat, Darlene?"

"Um... Meaty things."

Doctor Rule wrote down a few thing into his notebook. He then asked, "How does he get into your room, Darlene?"

"He comes in at night. I usually keep the window open, but sometimes, I have to get up to open it for him. He doesn't like it when I leave him outside. One time, he showed up while I was asleep, and he couldn't get in. The next night, he yelled at me for being stupid."

"He called you stupid?" asked the doctor curiously.

"He calls me a lot of mean names. He can't help himself. Wolves are just like that."

"I see," said the doctor with a nod. "Do these names ever upset you?"

Darlene sighed. She looked down at her own hands and fiddled about with her nails idly. "Sometimes. But I know why he does it. Wolves and humans aren't supposed to be friends. I think sometimes it gets to him. Wolves usually eat girls like me."

The doctor wrote down a few more notes and asked, "Do you think Shadow wants to eat you?"

"Oh, he already told me that. He said that the first time he came to see me, he was going to eat me."

"Why didn't he?"

"I touched his nose. It calms him down. He's been my friend ever since, and whenever he gets like he is going to do something bad to me, I just touch his nose… or hug him. He's mad when I do that, but he calms down afterwards."

"Are you ever afraid of him, Darlene?"

The girl thought about it. "I'm not afraid of Shadow. I love him."

"Does he love you?"

"No," she shook her head. "He's only my friend. He tells me often how much he hates me, but that doesn't mean anything. If he keeps coming to see me and I keep touching his nose, we'll always be friends whether he likes me or not. I belong to him. I made a promise. I won't break it."

Doctor Rule had never been so focused in all of his life. This was the strangest conversation he ever had with a child. It was fascinating. He, of course, did not believe a word of it; however, he knew that this would be one of the most challenging clients he would ever have.

Another thing that really surprised him was how intelligent she seemed at six years old. Darlene had mastered her wolf lore perfectly, and there were a number of distinct marks in it that the doctor saw as brilliant. Why would any child imagine a friend who hated them? Why would they accept it? Her answer was simple: It is just how wolves are.

Her creation of Shadow was not one of selfishness; it was one of imagination and creativity. Fully grown, she could very easily become a best-selling author. The problem was still the same, however. She thought it was real, and that needed to be dealt with. Doctor Rule already knew this would take time–possibly a year or more. He decided in that moment that he was ready for it.

Leaning forward in his chair, he smiled and looked into Darlene's eyes. He said to her, "I believe you."

"You do?" she asked–somewhat surprised.

"I do, and I want to hear more."

"Well, okay," she said with a smile. "I'll tell you everything."

Chapter 14 – First Impressions

Lucas was in the nearby bathroom brushing his teeth that night. Samantha was already in bed with a lot on her mind. The first session with Doctor Rule was now a couple of hours in the past, and she was thinking heavily upon the experience. "Lucas," she called to her husband.

Lucas spat into the sink and replied, "Something on your mind, dear?"

"What did you think of Doctor Rule?" she asked. "Are you sure he is the type that should be dealing with our daughter?"

Lucas did not answer right away. He busied himself with rinsing out his mouth first. Turning about, he said to her, "The man came with above and beyond the qualifications to deal with Darlene's little problem. You told me not to spare any expense, and I didn't. In fact, I was told by most of my fellow associates at the office that he might not even take her case on account that it was below his paygrade."

"But he did," she said.

Lucas walked over to the bed and sat down at the foot of it. He rubbed his wife's feet casually as he replied, "He did, and that is why we are about to lose an arm and a leg in what he is going to charge us. To be honest, I would have settled for someone cheaper simply for practical reasons, but you made it very clear that—."

Samantha pulled her feet back and interrupted, "She's our daughter!"

"I know that, dear, and I'm fine with this if you are. Just keep in mind that I'll likely be taking slightly longer shifts to pay for Doctor Rule. As far as what I think of him, I saw nothing wrong with the guy. He went out of his way to talk to us about the whole process. The very fact that a man of his acumen was interested in our daughter's problems likely means that he is the very man for the job. The imaginary wolf has to go–you know that, I know that, even Doctor Rule knew it."

Samantha released her feet from captivity, and Lucas resumed rubbing them. She sighed and squirmed a little before saying, "I've been a nervous wreck ever since she acted out that other day."

"That's why I'm rubbing your feet instead of making passionate love to you, dear."

She smirked at him. "Darlene was always such a sweet-natured girl."

Lucas remarked, "Doctor Rule actually said he considered Darlene to be smart beyond her age. I think I believe that. She's always done very well. Grade school is right around the corner, and I'll bet you anything, she'll be getting straight A's. We've always wanted a genius daughter, didn't we?"

"You wanted a boy," she said.

"I never once said that. I was going to be happy with whatever we'd have. I was equally fine with either sex–*especially* if it was a boy."

She pointed at him, "See?!"

"It was a joke, dear." Lucas saw her pouting and decided to crawl into bed with her. He said, "Besides, didn't you hear about her last physical?"

"No," she said grumpily. "I've been so preoccupied with all this that I've been distracted. Was it good?"

Lucas smiled and put an arm around her. "The doctor said that our daughter was the picture of health. He actually said that it would surprise him if she *could* get sick."

"Really?" she asked hopefully.

"Yep," nodded the father. "Said he never saw anything like it. Couldn't find a darn thing wrong with her. Not even a single blemish on her skin. I hadn't noticed that until he pointed it out. Our daughter is as healthy as an ox."

Samantha considered it. "Well, she's only been sick one time in her life. It was that cold she had last year." She paused and then jokingly remarked, "I think she once told me that Shadow would make it so that she couldn't get sick anymore."

"Well, at least that wolf is good for something," joked the husband.

Samantha nodded. "It is a funny coincident, isn't it? You know that thing they say in psychology classes?"

"What's that?" asked Lucas.

"Self-fulfilling prophecies. It's like a mental placebo that you give to yourself. You believe really hard in something, and then it ends up coming true."

"It sounds like self-delusion to me," murmured Lucas.

"Well, it was usually like that in the class I took. Usually, people could convince themselves that something was true to the point that it took over their lives. Maybe, in some way, that's what Shadow is. She believed a little too hard, and now, he is real to her in a way that even keeps her from being sick."

Lucas replied, "I'd rather her be sick once in a while rather than going crazy. You know, when I spanked her the other day, she screamed for a little bit and then just went stark quiet. There is something wrong about spanking a child that won't cry about it. I felt like an idiot."

"That sounds awful," whimpered Samantha.

"But it's true," returned Lucas. "The whole point of corporal punishment is to hurt the child enough to set them on a better path. You saw how Darlene acted; she deserved that spanking. But I swear that ten seconds into it, she went totally quiet. It was almost like she started to enjoy it. I think it was that moment that I really thought we needed to get the girl to a shrink and fast. Something isn't right about a girl who doesn't scream and cry when she's being spanked."

Samantha sunk down under her sheets some more. She was rather miserable from hearing Lucas talk this way. "I just hope you're doing what's best."

"Dear, you let me have the reigns, and I'm not going to give them back so easily. I'm going to see this through until we get our daughter back."

84

"I know. I know," Samantha said quickly. "Just promise me you're doing the right thing."

Lucas kissed his wife. "I promise."

"Okay," she replied halfheartedly.

Chapter 15 – Edward

Many weeks had passed. Darlene was finally going to grade school. Her sessions with Doctor Rule continued on a biweekly basis, and it seemed that the little girl had really started to look forward to them. Most of the sessions were one-on-one while Lucas and Samantha waited outside.

"Did you know wolves like to rip out a person's throat first?" asked Darlene the moment she was alone with Doctor Rule.

The doctor entirely held his composure and replied, "Do they? Why is that?"

"Shadow said that it's the quickest way to keep them from fighting back. It's everybody's weakness. You can't breathe, and blood goes everywhere. You can't live without your neck."

"Does Shadow say it just as you did?" asked Doctor Rule.

She nodded. "Shadow says whatever he wants to say. It's different than regular people. Regular people are always trying to say nice things unless they get angry. Wolves are always angry and full of hate. They don't care what they say. Shadow talks to me a lot about killing and eating. It's a wolf's favorite thing to talk about."

"Do you like hearing those things?"

Darlene looked down and kicked her feet idly. "No."

"Why haven't you told him to stop?"

"You can't tell a wolf not to be a wolf. Besides, he doesn't like anything I talk about, so it's only fair."

Doctor Rule smiled with fascination. He had never had such an interesting client before. He tossed back a few pages in his notebook and collected his thoughts. Finally, he said, "You said that you talk to him about your day and your friends. Do you talk to him about Cindy?" He watched her carefully.

"Oh, Cindy," shrugged Darlene. "Shadow doesn't care about Cindy. I'm starting to wonder about her myself."

"What do you mean?"

"Remember when I told you about her dragon friend–the one named Ozzie?"

"Yes."

Darlene leaned forward and whispered, "I'm starting to think that Ozzie is not even real."

"Why is that?" asked the doctor.

"She just keeps changing her story! Even Shadow knows it. He keeps bringing up how stupid the whole thing sounds. I mean… Can dragons make rainbows out of friendship or not?! And even if they could, what does that even mean? Shadow told me that that he thinks Cindy is out of her mind and probably deserves to be eaten."

Doctor Rule was writing stuff down faster than he could think. "Do *you* think that she should be eaten?"

"No! Never! She doesn't even belong to Shadow."

"And *you*... do?"

"I promised him," said Darlene with a nod.

"A quick off-topic question," said the doctor leaning forward. "Do you tell Shadow about our sessions?"

"Every time. Why?"

"What does he think of me?"

"He doesn't care about you."

"Do *you* care about me, Darlene?"

"Yes," she said with a nod. "You're a nice man. You let me talk about Shadow."

"And you are fine with Shadow not caring about me because…"

She finished for him, "Because a wolf can only be a wolf."

"Of course," said the doctor with a nod. He sat back with a fascinated air.

"Are you okay, Doctor Rule?" asked the little girl.

Doctor Rule nodded and replied, "I'm fine, Darlene. You know, I understand what is going on with Cindy and her dragon. You are probably correct that Ozzie is not real—what we call *imaginary*."

"Yes," Darlene said with a nod.

The doctor continued, "When I was young, I had an animal friend of my own who really seemed to me to be as real as Shadow."

"Who was it?"

"His name was Edward, and he was a three foot tall rabbit."

Darlene corrected, "Rabbits aren't that big."

"I know," said Doctor Rule with wide eyes. "That's what I told him, but he explained that he was a special rabbit that could grow bigger than the normal ones."

"Oh."

"Yes," smiled the doctor. "Like with Shadow, he came to see me every so often but was never around when people were near. He came to see me mainly in the school playground when I stepped behind an oak tree. As long as nobody could see me, Edward came out and began telling me how much he wished I was a bunny."

"Did you want to be a bunny, Doctor Rule?"

"I think I did. It had something to do with making chocolate, I think."

Darlene's eyes went wide. "That was the Easter Bunny! The Easter Bunny is named Edward?"

"Apparently," said the doctor with a chuckle.

The little girl could see that the doctor–in some ways–was being sincere, but there was still something weird about it. She said, "Well, if you still know him, you may want to keep him away from Shadow. Wolves eat rabbits."

"That they do," said the doctor looking over his notes. "I promise to keep him away."

"You still know him?"

"I don't see him as often as I used to, but yes."

Darlene sat there for a while trying to figure the doctor out. After some time, she leaned forward and said, "I believe you." Doctor Rule smiled. The seeds had been planted.

Chapter 16 – Progress

It was a private meeting between Doctor Rule, Lucas Peri, and Samatha Peri. Darlene was at school that day and knew nothing of the meeting, but this had been at the request of the doctor. "I'm very happy you've come," said Rule. "I'm sure you are both eager to know how things are progressing."

Lucas was the first to reply, "I hope we are not about to receive some bad news. We're paying you enough."

Samantha gave her husband a look and whispered, "Lucas, that was rude."

Doctor Rule smiled and raised a hand. "Please, Samantha, it's quite all right. Your financial situation has been a concern of mine as well. I wanted to speak to both of you as a way to confirm that you have not been wasting your money."

"Fair enough," said Lucas with a nod. "It has been a bit difficult to know anything since we have not been invited into the sessions. I've almost lost track of how long she's been seeing you."

"Eight months," replied the doctor respectfully. "Let me lay certain things on the line for you both. Your daughter, Darlene Peri, is on the very edge of becoming delusional." The parents looked at each other with much concern. Rule continued, "Right now, she is infatuated with a creature born of a childish imagination. It has become quite real to her. You have assured me that she had not had any negative influence so I can only conclude that this

Shadow is entirely the creation of Darlene, and she deeply desires to believe in him.

"Furthermore, your daughter seems to be a genius. Her manner and tone are beyond her age and seems to evolve and improve every time we meet. Her intelligence is boosting her ability to make her creation more plausible. There have been times where she has been so precise about Shadow that I wondered myself if he might be real; however, we all know that it isn't true.

"One of the recent attempts I have made to pull her away from her delusion is to tell her about my own imaginary friend, a bunny named Edward. She believes me to some extent because I am not really lying to her. I did grow up with the selfsame imaginary friend, and to this day, I still think about him. It was quite easy for me to converse about it, but I believe that a part of her knows the truth of him–which she is also beginning to see concerning her friend Cindy's dragon. I'm hoping that she will begin to understand that, as real as she has made Shadow, he is no more real than Edward or the dragon Ozzy."

Lucas waved his hand and broke in quite abruptly, "Doctor! Doctor, this is a lot to handle. Are you seriously certain Darlene is delusional?!"

"Not delusional. She's a vastly intelligent child who is choosing imagination over reality. The only other alternative would be if she was being fed the fantasy by a third party… or Shadow himself," he added jokingly, "and you have assured me that neither of these are the case."

Samantha was getting upset. "Is she going to be like this forever?"

Doctor Rule leaned forward and looked the mother in the eyes. "Miss Peri, I assure you that your trust in me is not misplaced. I am doing everything in my power to draw your daughter back into a less fanciful reality, but more so, I want her brains and intellect intact so that she can be an invaluable member of society. Your daughter is a genius; I am sure of it. I would ask you to encourage her to write stories when this is all through. She needs an *out* for this sort of imagination."

Seeing that Samantha was calmed from his answer, the doctor looked back at Lucas. He said, "Mister Peri, your daughter has been one of the most fascinating cases I've ever had to deal with, and I am taking this very seriously. I want you to understand that every penny you have been paying me has been worth it. I am making progress. This is simply not something that can be rushed."

Lucas nodded after making a long sigh. He put his arm around his wife and asked, "We just want Darlene to be okay."

"Naturally," said the doctor. "Now, do either of you have any questions?"

"How much longer?" asked Lucas.

"At least, another three months. She should be able to see reality properly before her seventh birthday." The husband took the news hard, yet he nodded.

Samantha spoke next, "This all started to go downhill when I gave her that Little Red Riding-Hood book. She carries it wherever she goes now. Is that a problem?"

The doctor smiled. "I agree that giving her that particular book may not have been the best thing to help her with this problem, but at this point, I'd recommend that you let her keep it. And let's have a little chat about that book. I looked through it and found it to be an edited version of Charles Perrault's tale. He was a seventeenth century French author who wrote a number of fairy tales–but likely none as provocative as this one.

"I must tell you that there are some unusual anomalies in this story that Darlene–with her stunning intelligence–has homed in on. Most children would miss them entirely, but this book has managed to solidify her relationship with her own big bad wolf to the point where she has suggested that she would not very much care if Shadow tried to eat her up.

"I know this is going to sound terrible, but Darlene's relationship with Shadow is a submissive one. She has told me on a number of occasions that she belongs to him. She has also suggested that Shadow hates her, yet she professes loyalty to him beyond measure. Even with Shadow being a figment of her imagination, this is unhealthy for her."

Lucas asked, "Then why not rid her of the book?"

"Because she would become enraged and turn her back to reality altogether. You would lose your daughter very quickly. She needs to understand the fallacy of the book along with the fallacy of the unreal–such as Shadow himself. All things unreal must be dismissed. That does not mean that she can stop enjoying them–as morbid as they maybe–but she must understand the difference between the real and unreal. The book needs to stay with her. If it is ever to be removed, she *must* do it herself."

Samantha was–at this time–holding onto Lucas' arm. The whole thing was very distressing to her. Lucas– keeping a strong front for her sake–said, "And you are going to make this happen?"

Doctor Rule placed his fingers together and spoke to the parents with the greatest of sincerity and intent, "I am the *only* man who can make this happen. You have been quite fortunate to obtain my services. I promise you that you will have your daughter back before she is seven. And at that time, she will finally understand that there is no such thing as the big bad wolf."

After the parents looked at each other for a short time, Lucas turned back to the doctor and said, "Very well. Do what you have to do." Doctor Rule gave him a reassuring nod.

Chapter 17 – The Death of Ozzy

Darlene had come into the room looking fairly glum. Doctor Rule watched carefully as she pulled herself up to the couch. In a sullen voice, she greeted, "Hi, Doctor Rule."

"Welcome back, Darlene," said the doctor. "Forgive me for saying so, but you *do* look a little upset today. You are usually a bit more chipper."

She nodded but did not actually explain it. The doctor remained quiet for a moment before asking, "Did you want to talk about it? You know that I'll listen to anything you have to say."

"I know," she said with another nod. "You're really good at that."

"Thank you," said Rule.

The girl released a dramatic sigh and spoke, "I had a sort of bad time with Cindy."

"Oh?"

"Well, we were hanging out at the park together, and she began talking about Ozzy. It was the same kinda stuff–you know, all that stuff that she keeps changing. I wasn't really saying anything."

"Why not?" the doctor asked.

Darlene made a quick shrug. Soon, she replied, "It just wasn't any fun anymore, I guess. I had told her all about Shadow, and I meant it. But she… Cindy was just making it up, and I knew it."

The doctor gestured to Darlene and said, "Something tells me she noticed how quiet you were."

"Yes," she groaned. "She asked me why I wasn't talking to her, and I told her because I wasn't in the mood. Cindy was all polite about it, but then I guess I got annoyed with the whole thing, and I told her that I didn't think Ozzy was real."

"How did she respond?" asked Rule.

"She didn't... at first. She just sort of frowned and wandered around for a little bit. I asked her what was wrong with her, and she told me I was being mean to her. I tried to explain why I told her that, but she still said I was being mean. I was really getting annoyed."

The doctor nodded and said, "It sounds like things were getting a bit heated between you two. I hope things didn't end too badly."

"No, it's okay, I guess," said Darlene. "I didn't really wanna be there anymore, but part of me wanted to fix it. We've been friends for as long as I can remember–not as long as me and Shadow though. Anyways, I explained to her that I didn't think Ozzy was real and that he was only imaginary."

"And she said?"

"She told me that if Ozzy wasn't real than neither was Shadow. Hearing that made me cry."

"Oh, dear," muttered the doctor.

"I cried because it was just hard to hear that, but when she saw me cry, she started to cry too, and we just started crying together. It was a little weird to me to go to a park and just start crying in the middle of it, but that's what we did."

Darlene kicked her feet a little and then continued, "She offered to hug me, and I hugged her back. We talked a little bit about Ozzy and Shadow. She said she thought that I knew it was just a game. She told me that she didn't even believe in Ozzy for a while. It was just something she liked to bring up with me so we could keep talking. She didn't know that I believed her."

Doctor Rule said, "So, there really is no Ozzy."

"There never was an Ozzy. He was imaginary this whole time. She said so."

The doctor nodded. "And what about you and Shadow?"

"Well, she thought that if she was making Ozzy up then I must be making up Shadow. I *really* wanted to tell her that Shadow was real, but… Well, it just wouldn't have been right."

Rule smiled knowingly. "You told her that Shadow was made-up as well."

"Yes. I had to! We might have stopped being friends!"

"No, I understand. You did what you had to do. Your friendship was at stake. Is everything all right between you two now?"

"It's fine. We just don't talk about Ozzy or Shadow anymore."

"That still doesn't explain why you looked so upset. If you and Cindy are doing well, then you should be quite pleased right now."

"Oh, I am very happy we are still friends. Cindy means a lot to me. I am upset because I feel like I betrayed Shadow."

The doctor noted her use of the word "betrayed." He asked her, "How was that a betrayal? I thought Shadow didn't care about Cindy."

"He doesn't care about anybody, but I love him and wanted to tell the world. It's hard though because nobody really believes in him. It's like you and Edward. How can anyone know they exist when they are always hidden? Edward only met you behind a tree, and Shadow only comes to me at night. As much as Cindy has seen him, Shadow might as *well* be imaginary."

"Mmhmm," hummed the doctor.

She went on, "I guess I'm upset because I feel like the whole world doesn't understand what I am going through with Shadow. How did you deal with your problems with Edward?"

The doctor had been prepared for the question, "Well, I suppose... at some point... I had to just move on."

"Move on?"

"There was more to deal with in life than dealing with a giant bunny. Nobody ever saw him, and as much as I would talk about him, nobody ever believed me. I had to just let him go."

She asked, "Was Edward even real?"

"He was to me. He still is. I've already told you much about him."

"You have," she said with a nod. "Is Edward imaginary?" she asked.

"He's real to me, Darlene."

The girl stared at the doctor intensely for a brief period before asking, "Do you think Shadow is imaginary?"

"I've never met him. You'd make the better call on that one. I can only speak for Edward."

"That makes sense. So, when you started moving away from Edward, did you feel like you betrayed him?"

"I did."

"And that's okay?"

"I had to deal with life. I had no choice."

Darlene looked down for a bit as if in deep thought. Finally, she said, "I know it's early but I kind of wanna go home now."

The doctor nodded and stood up. "Very well. See you in a few days?"

"Yes," she said pensively.

Chapter 18 – A Difficult Question

Darlene was in a thoughtful mood after coming home from school. She had not talked much to her parents which caught their attention. At the dinner table, she still remained quiet; however, she kept looking up at mother and father as if she wanted to speak.

Lucas–although uncomfortable–asked her, "Is there anything on your mind, sweetie?"

Darlene moved food around on her plate for a bit without answering. She cocked her head a few times in an almost playful way. This new sort of attitude was strange and unexpected to the parents. Samantha especially seemed provoked. Before Lucas could ask the question again, Darlene suddenly said, "I was wondering if I could ask you both something."

Samantha let out a quick sigh and said, "Of course, you can!" Lucas added a nod to his wife's reply.

Darlene continued to play with her food. Normally, this sort of behavior was discouraged, but the parents were allowing it temporarily. Darlene finally asked without looking up, "Do you think Shadow is imaginary?"

Samantha accidently dropped her fork onto her plate. It made a sudden and loud noise which gave both mother and father a start. Darlene was unfazed and continued to pick at her food. The situation had become awkward. They were unsure if they should discuss the topic or not. Doctor Rule had made it clear that he was dealing with it and that any move in the wrong direction could cause trouble for her.

Samantha froze up. She was too nervous to reply, so Lucas decided to try his luck. "Darlene, you haven't talked about Shadow in a while. Any reason you are bringing it up now?"

"I dunno," was all she said.

Lucas made a hard sigh as he stared at her for a short period. "Have you been discussing Shadow with Doctor Rule much lately?"

"Yes," she said with a little nod.

Samantha suddenly broke in with, "He's a very nice man, isn't he, Darlene?"

"I like him," said the little girl.

Lucas flashed his wife a look. It was painfully obvious that she had asked the question in a fit of nervousness. They already knew that Darlene liked Doctor Rule, so there was clearly no reason to ask her that. Still, he forgave her as he always did. Returning to Darlene, he asked, "What has Doctor Rule said about Shadow?"

Darlene responded, "He said that he doesn't really know Shadow personally. He knows that Ozzy the dragon is imaginary, and I think his bunny friend Edward is imaginary too. I was just wondering if you think Shadow is imaginary. That's all."

Samantha chimed in and said, "I know Shadow is very important to you, dear."

Lucas could not decide whether that was a good or bad thing for his wife to say. He was really hoping that she could keep from just throwing things out there. The father said to Darlene, "I've never met Shadow, Darlene."

"Doesn't mean he isn't real," said the girl.

"I suppose you're right, but if he doesn't make himself known, I'm happy to simply not believe in him. You've been talking about him for a long time, Darlene, and I have yet to see the wolf." Samantha was now glaring at her husband. As it happens, neither one of them knew if they were handling this well.

Darlene was quiet for a time. She ate some of her food and finally asked, "Does being imaginary mean that Shadow isn't real?"

Samantha took this one, "Of course, he's real, honey. He's real to you. Isn't that what's important?"

Lucas leaned over and whispered to his wife, "Dear, don't you have that thing to check on in the laundry room?"

"What thing?"

"That... *thing*," he persisted.

After a brief glare, the mother stood up and excused herself. Lucas leaned on the table and looked at his daughter. "Darlene, I really don't think Shadow is real. I don't mind that you made up a character that you really like, but if I never get to see him, then I just can't believe in him. So, yes, I think Shadow is just imaginary."

Darlene sighed and nodded. She muttered lightly, "That's what I was thinking."

"You were thinking what?" asked the confused father.

"Nothing," she replied indifferently.

"No... what did you say, Darlene?"

"Nothing," she repeated.

Lucas was getting frustrated; however, he did his best to remain calm. The father asked, "Do you think Shadow is imaginary?"

"I guess," she said. "I dunno. Maybe. I just liked him; that's all." She then began to eat what was on her plate rather furiously.

Lucas did not know what to make of it. It was good news, he thought; although, he was not sure if he had done something wrong. When it came down to it, he figured honesty was best; however, it did not seem right to keep on interrogating her while she was enjoying dinner.

Samantha came back in after doing that *thing*. She had really just been around the corner in the kitchen trying to listen in. After sitting back at the table, she held out her hand to Lucas. He took it, and they looked on at their daughter wondering how things were soon to turn out.

Chapter 19 – Confession

"The whole thing has been really confusing, I guess," said Darlene to Doctor Rule.

"I'm sure," said the doctor with a nod.

"I really thought he was real. He seemed so real. It was like I could touch him and everything. Does this even make sense?"

Doctor Rule smiled. "It makes perfect sense, Darlene. It was like that with Edward. There's nothing wrong with it. Imagination is a powerful thing, isn't it?"

"I guess so," she said kicking her feet a little. "Shadow had always been so important to me, and now, I guess I won't ever see him again. But then... I guess I've never really ever seen him. He was only in my head... like with Cindy and Ozzy."

Doctor Rule made a simple mark onto his notepad before replying, "Reality and imagination are meant to move hand in hand. You are a bright girl, and your imagination is highly developed. You should not simply walk away from Shadow as much as you should try and make something of him."

"What do you mean?" she asked curiously.

"Well... at school, do you ever draw pictures?"

"Sometimes."

"You could try drawing Shadow."

"But he isn't real."

"It doesn't matter. In many ways, he is still your friend. You can draw inspiration from him. There is no reason why you should avoid the things that you love. Shadow was your creation. Embrace him on a creative level. Make him real to other people."

"I guess I can do that," she said with a smile. "I've always liked showing people the pictures from my Little Red Riding-Hood book."

"I would suggest you draw your own from now on," said Rule. "I think you'll find it very satisfying."

"Okay," she said with a nod. "Can I tell my mom and dad now?"

"Are you sure?" he asked.

"I'm sure."

Doctor Rule smiled at the girl silently for a moment before standing up to open the door of his office. Soon, Lucas and Samantha were allowed into the room where they stood before their daughter. Everyone was silent for a bit. Darlene finally looked up at them and said, "Shadow isn't real. He was imaginary. I never really saw him or anything. I'm sorry for causing trouble."

Her confession came as a surprise to the parents; however, they were quick to respond. Both of them got down on their knees and hugged and kissed their child. Samantha said, "We love you very much, sweetie. It's all right that you had an imaginary friend. We have all had one growing up."

Lucas rubbed her back and added, "You're a very talented girl, Darlene. You're doing so well in school. We're very proud of you."

"Thank you," she said. "Doctor Rule said I can draw pictures of Shadow whenever I want. Is that okay?"

"That's fine, sweetie," said the mother. "Draw as many as you want. We'll pin them to the refrigerator." Lucas smiled but did not reply. He looked up at the doctor–who simply nodded in a confirming way.

Darlene hugged both of her parents again and told them, "I love you both so much. I won't make any more trouble again. I just wanna go home so I can think about all this."

"And your birthday is right around the corner," said Samantha. "You'll be seven. You're growing right up."

"I can't wait," said Darlene with a smile.

Lucas stepped over to Doctor Rule and quietly asked, "Are things really all right?"

Doctor Rule pulled the father away from his daughter and replied, "I believe so. I still wish to see her a few more times, but essentially, our sessions have come to an end. This was, after all, the goal of our sessions. She no longer believes in Shadow."

Lucas nodded. "So… she will be okay?"

"I believe so."

The father shook the doctor's hands and thanked him. "We appreciate everything."

"It was a pleasure," said Rule. "I suggest you take her home and assist this wonderful girl into her seventh year."

"Will do," said Lucas. "And once again, thank you."

Doctor Rule watched as the parents were leading Darlene to the front door of his building. He smiled with a certain amount of pride in which he felt for his profession. As Darlene was just about to go through the door, she gave the doctor a strange look. It felt something like regret... or was it defiance? It could have been both; it was rather confusing to interpret. In any case, it had been brief and a bit of a shock to the doctor. When the family had left him alone in his quiet office, he walked back to his room and looked through his notes. Running his hand through his hair, he struggled for a moment, wondering if something had been overlooked. Eventually, he resigned himself to success.

*****

Darlene had a pleasant dinner with her mother and father. She talked a little about Shadow; although, she always mentioned that he was her imaginary friend. She talked about all the pictures she was going to draw of him. "I've been practicing drawing at school anyways. I think if I keep doing it, I'll keep getting better."

Samantha said, "Practice makes perfect!"

"I'm proud of you, honey," said Lucas. "I want to see them when you finish."

"I'll make so many, the refrigerator will be covered in them."

Lucas chuckled, "As long as we can still get to our food." Everyone giggled.

Later that evening, Samantha was just putting Darlene to bed. The mother kissed Darlene on her forehead and said, "We love you very much, Darlene. You're a good girl."

"Thanks, mom," replied Darlene.

"I suppose you won't be spending the night with Shadow this time."

"No," said Darlene with a shake of her head. "He isn't real. But I'll draw pictures of him. Don't worry."

"Can't wait to see them. Good night, Darlene." And then she kissed her daughter again.

"Good night, mom." Samantha went to her door, looked once more upon her daughter, turned off the light, and then pulled the door shut.

Darlene lay perfectly still in the darkness. She waited patiently until she heard the scratching upon her window. Immediately, the girl got out of bed, pushed open the window, and calmly returned. Soon, she could see the glowing yellow eyes of a creature staring at her in the dark. The beast was resting calmly between her legs as it looked at her.

It spoke, "Did you do as I asked, Darlene?"

"I said everything you told me to say. Everyone now thinks that you were my imaginary friend–even Doctor Rule."

The yellow eyes moved close to the girl's face. His hot breath puffed over and over across her as she lay there very still. A satisfied snarl came from the creature's throat before she heard him say, "Good girl."

Chapter 20 – Halloween

Darlene was now seven. She was in the second grade and one of the school's brightest students. She never received any grade lower than an A. As she had promised, the girl was becoming quite the artist. She loved drawing wolves–especially the one she called Shadow. Her teacher would constantly praise her for her artistic skill–which seemed far more advanced for a girl of her age.

At home, she was always a very warm and polite personality. She did not talk about Shadow anymore unless it was in reference to her drawings or in an explanation of her past imaginary friendship. Speaking of conversation, Darlene's vocabulary also seemed to have evolved to a degree. Lucas bought his daughter a fancy dictionary in hopes that she would learn even more words as to expand her horizons. She promised to look through it from time to time; however, she still greatly loved her copy of *Little Red Riding-Hood* and read that with a regularity.

Although Cindy was still Darlene's friend, a strange divide had been steadily forming between them. There was nothing forced about it. Both girls seemed to simply get preoccupied by other people and things. They were still friends, and they had even promised each other that; however, it was clear that their relationship had been suffering for a while. Darlene made little effort to fix the situation other than a few reassurances that they were still friends.

Darlene's creative endeavors seemed to be her focus. She would still work with other children when asked to, and she did this very well; however, there were very few connections made between her and them–if any at all. To be short, Darlene was popular without really making friends, and she seemed quite fine with this.

Halloween was coming up, and for some reason, Darlene had been looking forward to it for a number of months. She had never really cared much for the holiday until this particular year. Somehow, it was special to her this time, and she wanted to go all out for it. Samantha took her to a store to buy her whatever she wanted, and what Darlene wanted was a quite a lot.

Everything had to be *Little Red Riding-Hood* themed. She wanted even to dress up as the main character of her favorite story. A basket was also a necessity. Although Samantha did not understand why, Darlene also asked for a doll which looked like an old woman. The girl explained that it was Little Red's grandmother. When asked if she wanted to get a wolf too, Darlene declined.

On the night of Halloween, Darlene came out of her room in full costume. Samantha and Lucas stood side-by-side and smiled as she would show off. She skipped around the foyer with a smile and said, "I'm off to grandmother's house with my bun and butter! I hope I don't run into the Big Bad Wolf!"

The parents clapped, and Samantha said, "I'd watch out if I was you."

Lucas pulled out a wolf mask from behind his back and quickly placed it upon his face. "Gonna getcha!" he growled. Darlene screamed and ran around the room while her father chased her. Samantha laughed and quickly ran to get her camera. By the time she came back, father appeared to be goofily devouring her while Darlene was laughing.

Samantha took the opportunity to snap several pictures just to hold onto that happy scene.

Darlene skipped the entire night in front of her parents as she went hunting for candy. Every time she saw someone wearing a wolf mask, she would walk up and initiate a role play with them–generally following a scene from her favorite book. Some wolves would shy away from her, and others would play the role back for her. One of the wolves growled and began chasing her; however, this was promptly put to a halt by Lucas.

Darlene had never seemed so happy. To the parents, it felt surreal. Darlene had never really acted this way before. She seemed as if she was in another world. The candy did not really seem to mean as much to her. Darlene was hunting for wolves. Nevertheless, Lucas and Samantha allowed her to have her fun. This was a special day when children could pretend to be something they were not.

Darlene ended up with so much candy that she really could not keep going. Her basket was full. It signaled the end of the night, and the three ended up walking back to where they had parked the car. "I nearly got eaten!" cried Darlene as she jumped into the car. "Quick! We got to get home before the wolves get me!" She was giggling madly after saying this.

Samantha looked back at her after putting on her seatbelt. "I don't think I've seen you have so much fun, sweetie."

"I love Halloween," came the reply.

Lucas put the car into gear and started off for home. He said, "You do need to be careful though. You ran into the shadows a few times, and we almost lost sight of you."

"I'm sorry, dad. I was having too much fun. You heard what mom said."

Samantha nodded. "You'll have candy for a long time. Don't get yourself sick."

"Do you want it?" asked Darlene unexpectedly.

Both parents asked, "What?"

Darlene explained, "I guess I can have some of it, but I don't really need it."

"Neither do we," said the father honestly.

"It's okay," said the girl looking at her full basket. "I'll pass some out at school tomorrow."

Samantha smiled, "That's nice of you, sweetie."

Darlene was quiet for the rest of the drive home. She was smiling though as she looked out of the window. There was a certain giddiness to it that neither parent could understand, but they were glad that she had enjoyed herself.

That night–after Darlene had been put to bed, Darlene got up and began setting up a scene in her room. She took the grandmother doll and laid it upon the bed. She then went and put her Little Red Riding-Hood costume back on. She heard a sound and looked to her bedroom window. Shadow was sitting before it and gazing at her in his usual silent way.

"Shadow!" she said with a smile. "We're going to have a good time tonight."

118

"Why are you dressed like that?" he asked with something of a sneer.

"Don't worry; you're going to love it. We're going to play a little game, and at the end of it... you're going to devour me." She had said those words with a giggle. Shadow looked more confused than anything; however, he was entirely interested in whatever it was she had planned.

"Tell me about this game," he ordered her.

Chapter 21 – The Game

"We're going to act out the scenes from *Little Red Riding-Hood*," said Darlene to Shadow. "I'm going to be her, and you'll be... yourself. You're Master Wolf."

Shadow cocked his head slightly as she said this. He did not answer; although, it was extremely evident that he was paying attention. Darlene pointed to her bed where the grandmother doll was laying. "That's grandmamma. I had to use a doll for her. My real grandmother would probably not let you eat her."

Shadow remarked, "She would not need to."

"Well, that's true, but I only have the doll tonight."

The wolf looked at it briefly before turning his attention back to the girl. He asked, "Are you intent on allowing me to devour you? Stupid girl, it would mean your death."

"It's only a game, Shadow," she said playfully. The wolf snorted. She added, "Don't you like me in red?" The seven-year-old spun around with a smile.

The wolf replied with a guttural growl, "*I do*."

Darlene curtsied and then said, "We'll skip the part where we meet in the woods. Go to the door and pretend to be me coming to see my grandmother with your bun and butter."

"Must I leave your bedroom?" asked Shadow. "I am uninterested in an encounter with your parents."

"Just pretend you're outside. It's just a game, Shadow."

"Where will you be?"

"Just pretend I'm not here. I have to do Grandmother's voice."

"Very well," said Shadow as he walked to the door.

Darlene put the bedsheet over the doll and mimicked the voice of an old woman, "Who is it?!"

The wolf made no attempt to sound like Darlene when he replied, "It is I, your granddaughter, Little Red Riding-Hood! I brought you a bun and a little pot of butter that my mother has sent."

Darlene recognized that Shadow had said the exact lines from the book. He really had memorized it well. She responded in kind, "Draw back the peg back, and the bar will fall."

"Now, what do I do?" asked Shadow.

The girl replied, "You can come in now and tear Grandmother to bits." Shadow casually walked in, hopped up onto the bed, and regarded the doll. He noticed Darlene was watching very intently. After a pause, the wolf placed a claw down upon the lower part of the doll, bit deeply into the face and neck, and began ripping it apart with amazing strength. Fluff started to puff out of the seams as he slowly and methodically ripped Grandmother up. When he had finished, the doll was an unrecognizable pile of fabric and fill. Shadow returned his gaze to Darlene and asked, "And now what?"

Darlene released a sudden breath that she had been holding. "Get rid of the body and take her place. I'll come in when you're ready."

Shadow simply knocked the destroyed Grandmother off of the bed with a casual swat. He tucked his head under the sheet, crawled under it entirely, and turned about until only his head was showing. Darlene ran over to the door and knocked on the nearby wall.

The wolf asked, "Who is it?"

The reply, "It is I, your granddaughter, Little Red Riding-Hood! I brought you a bun and a little pot of butter that my mother has sent."

"Draw back the peg back, and the bar will fall," said Shadow.

Darlene made the motions with her hand and walked over to the bed. There was a moment where wolf and child stared at each other with absolute silence. Darlene looked oddly excited, but the wolf appeared more wary. It was as if he was uncertain what was about to happen. Nevertheless, the wolf spoke, "Put the bun and the little pot of butter on the chest, and come get into bed with me."

There was another long pause. Darlene made the motions of putting her things away and then proceeded to disrobe in front of the wolf. After this was finished, she pulled back the sheet and crawled into bed with Shadow. All the while, she stared into his eyes as if she could not look anywhere else. Shadow unconsciously licked his chops.

Darlene's next words were spoken softly as she continued to look deeply into his intense, yellow eyes. "Oh grandmamma, what long arms you have."

Shadow's breathing intensified. He replied, "All the better to hug you with, my dear."

The girl continued, "Oh grandmamma, what long legs you have."

Shadow's breath was now being mixed with a low growl which became audible with every exhale. He returned, "All the better for running with, my dear."

Darlene held up her young hand which immediately garnered the attention of the growling wolf. He looked at the hand as if it was the most fascinating thing in the room. She continued, "Oh grandmamma, what big ears you have."

Shadow's deep grow was turning into a snarl. He licked his chops as he gazed at her hand. Darlene knew he could see the blood flowing inside of it. It was like dangling meat in front of a wild animal. He replied, "All the better to hear you with, my dear."

"Oh grandmamma," she continued, "what big eyes you have."

"Darlene," he said with a trembling anger.

"Go on," she said sweetly as she waved her hand back and forth.

Shadow was regularly snarling now, and it was very noisy. Spittle was being tossed at Darlene as he did this, yet he still managed to say, "All the better to see you with, my dear."

Darlene placed two fingers on top of the wolf's snout and walked them around like two little legs. The wolf stared at them still, trembling with lust. He snapped a few times and was a constantly snarling so much that he was nearly foaming at the mouth. The girl was breathing deeply as she played with him like this. She was enjoying every moment of it. The attention she was getting was the most thrilling she had ever experienced.

And then finally, she said it: "Oh grandmamma…"

"Yeeees," growled the wolf.

She slowly moved her fingers down to his nose and said, "What great big teeth you have."

Shadow suddenly snapped out and bit Darlene's hand extremely hard. His teeth punctured her skin with so much pressure that one of the bones cracked, and she felt it. Darlene screamed and yanked back her hand as soon as the wolf released it. Shadow was huffing in a confused state. It was as if he had no idea where he was or what he was doing.

Darlene did not cry. She held the wrist connected to the wounded hand and watched as blood began gushing from the holes. She easily realized that she needed to go to the hospital for this. "Oh, my god," she said trembling. "Shadow, you got to get out of here."

"Right," he groaned falling out of the other side of the bed. The wolf blundered into a few things as he made for the open window, disappearing into the night.

Darlene was in a panic. There was no way to explain the bite in her hand. She looked around her room with desperation as she put her costume back on to cover her nudity. There was a glass cup sitting on her table which was half filled with water. She picked it up and smashed it into the table. After taking a deep breath, the girl grabbed as much of the shards of glass as she could… and then she screamed.

Samantha and Lucas were soon in the room and witnessed their daughter crying her heart out with her hand a bloody mess. "It hurts!" she cried. "I accidently knocked it over, and when I tried to pick it back up…"

The mother was horrified as she looked it over. "We need to get you to the hospital right now."

"I'll get the keys," said Lucas already on the move. "Don't touch her hand!"

"Come on, we need you to get up, Darlene," said Samantha trying very hard to keep her cool. She knew she was going to lose it later, but now was not the time. Darlene followed orders as she cried from the terrible pain. No one even noticed the animal bite.

Chapter 22 – Doctor Winston

Doctor Nathaniel Winston had been working at the local hospital for over fifty years. He was likely the most respected individual there, and much of that respect stemmed from the fact that he had seen it all. There was very little in the world of medicine that he had not touched in his lifetime; however, there was one patient that had the medical veteran fairly baffled. Her name was Darlene, and she had been brought in for having been severely lacerated by broken glass.

The girl had fallen into unconsciousness by the time she had been brought in, and she was immediately made the top priority. Doctor Winston was the man in charge of the operation, and he made sure the parents understood that she would–in all likelihood–be fine due to their rapid response. Hearing those words were certainly comforting to the parents, but they still spent every hour in the waiting room on edge.

Samantha was especially fragile in those moments; however, she never broke down. Lucas was a constant verbal support for her. He never let up in his efforts to calm her nerves, and it was working. "It was just an accident," he told her.

"How?" she asked with heavy breathing. "How did it break? It's not that far down to the floor."

"Honey, accidents happen. Don't beat yourself up. The doctor said she is going to be fine."

"He didn't say that *exactly*," she whimpered.

Lucas held his wife closely and allowed her to lean into him. He added, "The doctor will fix her right up. She's a strong girl. It'll take a lot more than glass to ruin her life, and you know that." The mother only nodded as her head was pressed against him.

Throughout the night, they received updates, and each one was more hopeful than the last. She was going to be fine, and all they had to do was wait until the hand was stitched up. Before they were allowed to see Darlene, Doctor Winston asked if he could see the couple in private. They agreed.

The parents were led into a small office, and everyone took a seat. The doctor regarded them without any amount of emotion for the first half of a minute. It was a rather odd thing to do, and it confused Samantha and Lucas to no end. Finally, Lucas asked, "You had something you wanted to talk about, Doctor?"

The doctor looked at him directly the moment he was addressed. It was beginning to look like Doctor Winston was there to examine the parents more than talk. He had a certain glare that was piercing. The parents had not noticed this glare when they had first met him with all the urgency going on.

Samantha–who was getting quite agitated with the man–leaned over and asked, "Is there something wrong with Darlene?"

Doctor Winston finally spoke, "You both informed the nurse when she was brought in of the circumstances surrounding your daughter. I looked through the report while I was patching the girl up."

128

"What about it?" asked Lucas.

The doctor had a habit of glaring directly at whoever addressed him last for a few moments. It was an irritating habit to the two parents. The doctor continued, "You told the nurse that she had been put to bed after going trick-or-treating, and sometime after this, she accidently knocks over a glass and mistakenly tries to pick it up. This was why her hand had been lacerated."

"Yes, that's what happened," said Samantha nervously.

The doctor nodded, but then he asked, "And what about the dog bite?"

The question only confused the parents. Lucas asked, "Dog bite? What dog bite? What are you talking about?"

Doctor Winston regarded the father gravely. "I know a dog bite when I've seen one. The glass was one thing, but the dog bite will have her in a cast for six weeks—not to mention the rabies shot I had to administer. My question is why you are both acting like you know nothing about it."

Lucas and Samantha looked at each other for a moment. They were incredulous. Lucas explained, "We don't have a dog. Darlene wasn't around any animals for the whole night. We were with her the whole time."

Samantha added, "I tucked her into bed. Her hand was fine. Doctor, that couldn't have been a dog bite. You saw all the glass."

"Yes, I did," said the doctor coldly. "And that sort of injury is not to be confused with the bite of an animal. You see, Mister and Missus Peri, she has clearly been bitten by a canine so hard that it has fractured the metacarpal bone in her right hand. This is no joke."

Lucas was getting annoyed. "You think we're joking with you? That's our daughter!"

"Correct," said the doctor glaring back at the father. "And for some reason she has been bitten by an animal without you knowing it, and furthermore, your account about the glass came directly from her. I understand that you were not there to witness it… and had her to explain it to you. Now, I have a ton of paperwork every time I have to perform operations like this, and to be perfectly honest, I have no idea what I am supposed write in it."

"You really think we're hiding something, don't you?" said Samantha. Lucas was getting a bit too angry to keep arguing.

The doctor replied to her, "I don't know what is going on to be honest. All I know is there is a piece of this puzzle that is clearly missing. It isn't really my job to tell you how to be parents, but one thing is certain, that girl was bitten quite viciously by an animal, and neither she nor her parents seem to know anything about it.

"I've been in this work for a long time, and I know when something just doesn't smell right. People come in here all the time with false stories hoping that the doctor won't find out. From talking to you both, I get the feeling that you are both just as in the dark as I am. So who does that leave?"

Lucas growled out the words, "Darlene is not a liar!"

"With all due respect, Mister Peri, there is no way that Darlene would not know about that bite."

"So what are you suggesting, Doctor? Are you saying she tried to cover up an animal bite by stabbing her hand with glass?! Are you insane?!"

Samantha held her husband's arm and whispered, "Lucas, calm down."

The doctor glared. "In a moment, I'll let you in to see Darlene so that you can take her home. She is in a cast and seems to be in fairly good spirits considering her episode. But before you see her, allow me to give both you a piece of advice off the record."

Although Lucas' ire was up, he allowed the doctor to speak, "Something happened to Darlene. It may not be easy to see or understand, but it is there regardless. Whether you want to believe in it or not, the thing will still persist until it will evolve into some manner of climax. I encourage you not to take my words lightly. I have had decades of experience with similar situations like this. It is not a realm for the closed-minded.

"Darlene is your daughter, and she *does* need you. She needs you in every way you can imagine. If she really is lying to you–and I think she is–then this is merely a very small sign of something terrible. Do you understand me?"

Lucas had calmed down some during the doctor's speech, but he was still upset from before. Even so, he replied, "Thank you for your advice, Doctor."

"Yes, thank you very much," added Samantha.

With that, Doctor Winston stood up and said, "Come with me. Darlene is looking forward to returning home." The parents followed him down the hall to where Darlene was waiting for them.

Chapter 23 – A Dark Performance

Darlene was in a cast, and her hand was heavily bandaged. Apart from this obvious fact, she was in good spirits as had been suggested by Doctor Winston. "I'm okay!" were her first words as soon as she saw her parents walk through the door. They smiled and were, at once, relieved to see that she was showing such good and healthy signs of recovery. The doctor–although present–remained silent and out of their way.

"I'll never bring water to bed again," she told them. "I still can't believe I did that. It was horrible!"

Samantha suggested, "Plastic cups from now on."

"As clumsy as I am, you never know," said Darlene jokingly. "If anyone could cut herself on plastic, it would be me, right?"

The mother giggled and replied, "Only you."

The girl looked up at her father and asked, "Are you mad at me, dad?"

Lucas realized that he had not been smiling much. He promptly did so and leaned down to hug her–careful not to bump her cast. "I'm happy you're better, sweetie."

"Thank you, dad," she said cutely. When Lucas stood back up, he noticed the cold stare of Doctor Winston on him. It only irritated the father.

Lucas looked back at Darlene and said, "Let's get you back home. We'll pick up some fast food on the way."

"Great!" she shouted as if full of energy. Lucas made a concerted effort not to look at the doctor on the way out of the hospital. Even so, he could not get the man's words out of his head.

As promised, the family picked up fast food and took it back to their house. They all sat around the table eating their fill. Darlene was struggling eating with her left hand, and Samantha helped her the first couple of times. "I can do it," said the girl with a giggle.

All the while, Lucas was quiet and thoughtful. He really should have been sleepy. They all somewhat were. They were still on a high from the events of the night. The problem with Lucas was that he did not think he could sleep if he wanted to. His mind was rushing like the wind. The man finally excused himself from the table and left without eating much from his plate.

Lucas calmly stepped into Darlene's bedroom. He stopped just inside of the door to have a look around. The window was pushed open–something Darlene did a lot. There was blood on the bed. Those sheets needed to be replaced, he thought. He walked over and pulled them from the mattress, but when he was folding them up, he noticed the little pieces of glass on the floor.

The father kicked some of them away with his shoes so that he did not accidently step on any of it. He leaned to the side to see if there was anything out of the ordinary. Lucas saw some cotton scattered about just under the bed. Carefully, the man leaned down and reached under the bed and pulled out… *a thing*. He was not sure *what* it was.

It was a horrendously torn piece of colored fabric covered in cotton that was falling all over the floor as he examined it. He was baffled as to why something like this was shoved under her bed. And then… Lucas saw a face. He had to place parts of the fabric together to see it, but there it was. He saw the face of an old woman and suddenly realized that this had once been some kind of doll.

Lucas called for Samantha, and she showed up soon after. "What is it?" she asked.

"You recognize this thing?" He showed it to her.

The mother cocked her head for a moment but then gasped, "That's Darlene's grandmother doll. I bought it for her when we were shopping for her Halloween costume. What in the world happened to it?"

"I don't have a clue, but I'm dying to ask her about it. How's she doing?"

"Well, she's great," said the mother. "I've never seen her so happy. It's almost like she doesn't even care that she got hurt."

"Nothing about a dog?" he asked.

Samantha grimaced. "No… but do you really think the doctor was right about that?"

"I dunno," said Lucas flatly. He then handed her the bedsheets and walked out to see his daughter.

When Lucas walked into the dining room with the destroyed grandmother doll, Darlene plainly looked as if she was seeing a ghost. "Oh, you found it," she said nervously.

"What is it?" he asked. Samantha walked in quietly behind him.

Darlene seemed at a loss for a moment. Soon, she explained, "That was a grandmother doll that my mother bought me. I… I tore it up because it happened in the story. I guess I shouldn't have done that, huh?"

Samantha broke in, "Honey, I didn't buy it for you to tear up. When did you do this?"

"A couple of days ago," she lied. "I shouldn't have done it. Am I grounded?"

"Well… no," said Samantha.

"Maybe," said Lucas sitting down across from his daughter.

"Maybe, dad?" asked Darlene.

The father looked his daughter in the eyes and said, "Darlene, you remember Doctor Winston, right?"

"Yes," she said with a nod.

"He told us that he found an animal bite on your hand." Darlene seemed confused. Lucas continued, "He said that it looked like a dog bite, and he was very sure of it. He even said that it was the reason one of your bones was fractured."

"But how?" she asked. "It was only glass."

Lucas rubbed his face with his right hand with complete frustration. He had never felt so awkward in front of a little girl before–let alone his daughter. He asked, "Have any dogs crawled in through your bedroom window–any you haven't told us about?"

"Dogs?" she asked incredulously.

"If you tell us, we won't be mad. It's just a question. We love you, Darlene."

Samantha sat next to her husband and whispered to him, "Honey, you look like you have a headache."

"I do," he grumbled.

Darlene frowned, and for a moment, she sneered. "Why would I lie to you?" she asked as if hurt. "It was just glass. The doctor must be stupid or something."

"Honey," groaned Lucas, "we're just trying to figure this whole thing out. We're not mad at you."

"You sound mad," she whimpered. "Is this because I leave my window open? I can keep it closed if you want. I don't want my own mom and dad to think I'm in danger."

Samantha broke in, "No, no, sweetie! We don't mind that you like the window open. It's just that the doctor really seemed to think that you were bitten by a dog, and we don't remember seeing you with a dog, honey."

"You don't believe me?" she asked. "Why would I lie about something like that? I got my hand cut up and everything, and you're worried about a dog bite that probably wasn't even there?"

Samantha looked at Lucas who was holding his head firmly. The man was doing his best trying to figure out what was going on. Nothing made sense to him. The whole thing was wreaking havoc on his brain, causing him pain. The torn-up doll had only made it more complicated. However, Lucas dearly wanted to trust his daughter. She had been nothing but cheerful since they had left the hospital. He missed that.

Lucas said to her, "Darlene, we aren't trying to put you on the spot or anything. We're just worried. It is entirely possible Doctor Winston just got something wrong. The only thing I want to know is if you're all right."

The girl's mood lightened some. "I'm fine, dad."

"If something bad was happening to you… you would tell us, wouldn't you? You trust us, right?"

"Of course," said Darlene. "I love both of you. Gosh, I'm so sorry I made you worry like that. I promise you that it was just the glass that cut me. I don't know why the bone broke, but it might be when I dropped my whole weight on it. They really seemed like they went in deep."

Lucas covered up his face with both hands letting his fingers dig into his hair. He mumbled, "All right. I believe you."

"Me too, sweetie," said Samantha. "You've always been a good girl."

Darlene held out her one arm. "Hug?" Lucas and Samantha nodded and stood up to hug their daughter. While they were unable to see her face, Darlene smirked.

Chapter 24 – Finality

It had been a few days before Darlene had seen Shadow again. She had expected the absence because of her hand being hurt. Shadow preferred Darlene always be at her best, but it was not possible while she was undergoing recovery. Even though she was not yet out of her cast, Darlene noticed Shadow sitting by her window on the present night. Only his yellow eyes were showing, but it was enough to let her know that he was there.

"Shadow?" she said.

"Darlene," said the wolf from the darkness. "We need to talk."

She leaned over and turned on her lamp so that she could see him. "I'm still in a cast. After you bit me, I—."

"I know what you did," he interrupted her. "Your hand has already healed; nevertheless, you should continue to keep the cast on until they tell you to remove it."

"They said I had to wear this thing for weeks." She poked at her hand. The discomfort was entirely gone.

The wolf crawled up onto her bed and stared at her. Darlene looked him in his cold eyes and asked, "Are you mad at me?"

"I am not angered by you, Darlene," said Shadow. "I simply came here to explain what has occurred between you and me."

"Something happened?"

"Indeed. We shall never be the same."

"Are we still friends?"

"As you wish," he replied.

"Then what's different?"

The wolf came closer to the girl and said with an eerie calmness, "I have tasted your blood, Darlene."

She cocked her head. "So?"

"Understand that what I am about to tell you has never been true until this moment. There will come a day in your life when–at the time of my choosing–I will kill you and devour your body. You cannot change this. You are my prey, and I am your master."

Darlene took the news as if she had somehow already known it. "I love you, Shadow."

"And I accept your love," he said in reply.

"You do?" she asked.

"I do. I accept your love as well as your life. Your life is mine, Darlene. I always finish what I start, and I have quite started on you."

"Why don't you finish me then?" she asked curiously.

"I am not in a hurry," he explained. "Darlene, I have been alive for a very long time. I have developed a patience of which stupid, little girls such as yourself could not comprehend."

Out of curiosity, the girl asked him, "Are you the same wolf from *Little Red Riding-Hood*?"

"I am," he confirmed. "Although the story is different than the real events, I still own them. I owned her, and now, I own you. Everything you are and ever will be belong to me for my own pleasure and personal consumption. Even your soul is forfeit. You are no longer a human of this world; you are *meat*. Do you understand this, Darlene?"

"I think so," she replied. "I always sort of thought that you might eat me someday. I just don't know what you're waiting for?"

"Are you in a hurry to die?" he asked.

"I was just curious."

"Darlene, hear me: I tasted your blood… and it was *sweeeeet*. But it can be sweeter still. I have not come to see you night after night to have it all end in a trifle. No. The time of my choosing is paramount. Until that day, I shall be your friend and accept your love as always, but understand me, you belong to no one else but me. No one else may devourer you but me. Your path is set, and there is no going back."

Darlene stared at him silently for a couple of minutes. Suddenly, she reached up and began rubbing his nose. The touch had absolutely no effect on him at all. He simply continued to stare at her. For the first time, Darlene was feeling awkward at touching his nose and promptly put a stop to it. Soon after, she became annoyed and snapped, "I don't care if you eat me! I love you!"

"Good girl," he replied calmly.

"I *wanted* you to taste my blood!"

"It was delicious," said the wolf.

"Did you come here just to make me afraid?"

Shadow lifted his head at the question. It seemed to interest him. "Darlene, you have never been afraid of me a day in your life."

"I'm not afraid of you. I *love* you. I really do love you! You're everything to me. I would do anything for you, even if it meant you would eat me."

The wolf nodded but said, "You have an interesting perspective, girl. You seem to believe that you have a say over whether I have the privilege of devouring you or not. Answer me this: If you were to touch my nose and forbid me from eating you in the next moment, would that really be enough to stop me?"

"You won't do it because you love me."

"Ah! But you seem to be getting confused. I never said that I loved you, Darlene. I have *hated* you, but I have never loved you."

"Do you hate me now?" she asked.

"I do not hate you anymore. I do not love you either. You will provide me a very delicious meal when I chose to tear that lovely throat out."

"I'm not afraid," she said with a pout.

Once again, the wolf nodded and replied, "There will come a day when you *shall* fear me, Darlene, and on that day, I shall kill you." The girl glared at the wolf defiantly. He added, "But until then, I shall be pleased simply to accept your love."

She crossed her arms and looked away. "Well, I *do* love you."

Shadow lied down upon the foot of her bed and replied, "Good girl."

Chapter 25 – A Very Good Girl

Nine years passed by. Lucas yawned as he hobbled into the kitchen. "Good morning, dear."

Samantha had just began making coffee. She smiled seeing her husband. "Good morning, Lucas. Still sleepy?"

He plummeted down into a chair and replied, "I don't understand what it is about sleeping that makes a man sleepy. I ought to be fine after all that."

"You're probably just not getting enough sleep, honey. You want coffee?"

"I would love coffee."

"Do you love coffee more than me?" she teased him.

"Depends. Is the coffee prettier?"

"Lucas!" she wined. He just chuckled at the fact that his wife had become jealous of his coffee.

After he had his cup, the father asked, "Darlene isn't up yet?"

Samantha shook her head. "She likes to *snooze* her alarm. I'm going to wake her up shortly."

Lucas nodded. "Hard to believe she's almost out of high school. It shouldn't be a surprise to me, but which one of us suspected she'd skip a grade?"

"It sure wasn't me," said Samantha, "but it does make sense. She's really smart, and all the other kids really like her. I don't even remember the last time she got anything less than an A."

Lucas smiled. "I think there was one B, and it was a B+. It was one of those fancy math classes, I think."

The mother sighed. "Oh, honey, those classes are rigged."

"They are?" asked Lucas.

"Either that or the teacher graded on a curve or something. I saw what she did, and she totally deserved an A+."

"You understood what she wrote?"

"No, but it looked very professional. She used colored ink for all the different numbers and everything. She should have gotten credit for *that*, at least."

Lucas chuckled and took another sip of coffee. "You know, I was thinking. When was the last time Darlene was sick?"

Samantha answered right away, "Last year, wasn't it?"

"No, that was you, dear."

"The year before that then?"

He shook his head. "That was me. Darlene even helped take care of me, and she never caught it."

Samantha sighed as she tried to remember. "The only time I remember her sick was a cold she had when she was really young. I can't remember what age it was though. Four or five."

146

"That can't be all," said the incredulous father.

"Well, you know what the doctors always say about her. She's the healthiest thing they ever did checkups on. Half the time, I think they want to put a blue ribbon on her."

Lucas chuckled for a moment. "Well, our daughter is not only smart; she's super healthy. What's wrong with that?"

"And she is beautiful," said Samantha beaming with pride.

"Oh, yeah," agreed Lucas. "I always worry that her beauty will go to her head, but she doesn't seem the type. She's a real egghead when it comes down to it–all those books she reads."

Mother added, "She still loves the book I gave her when she was little. Sometimes, I think she enjoys imagining herself as Little Red Riding-Hood even at sixteen."

"Well, that explains the jacket with the red hood on it," said father.

"You're just now noticing that?" she asked.

"Honey, you know I don't pay attention to what you girls wear."

She rolled her eyes. "She really never let that book go. It's all faded and falling apart, but she still takes it around with her." Samantha became a tad sullen.

Lucas noticed this and asked, "Are you okay, dear?"

"Just thinking. It's really nothing. Darlene really loves us, right?"

"Of course, she does. She reminds us of it all the time."

"Oh, I know. It's just... I guess if you hear something often enough, it loses some of its meaning."

Lucas was perplexed. "What are you talking about?"

"Well, when she says she loves us, do you think she means it?"

"Why wouldn't she mean it? We've always been there for her, haven't we? If you think of it, we pretty much did everything by the book. How could we have gone wrong?"

"Maybe, we didn't. I guess I am just a little worried to see her go."

"College?" he asked.

"Yes."

"Well, she has to get through high school before that. Why don't we go wake her up?"

"All right," Samantha said with a smile.

They both walked to the sixteen-year-old's bedroom. Samantha tried the door, but it would not open. She sighed and said, "I'll never get used to her locking the door. I don't care how old she gets."

"I know what you mean," he said.

Samantha called, "Darlene, you have school in an hour! Time to get up!"

A voice returned, "All right. Just give me a sec' to get dressed."

"All right," said Samantha. She looked at her husband for a moment before they both returned to the kitchen.

In the bedroom, a beautiful, young, teenage girl rolled over and lay her arm around the body of a large wolf. "Good morning, Shadow," she cooed.

"Mmhmm," he mumbled not even looking at her.

"I love you," she said.

"Yeah," he replied slowly getting up and away from her.

Darlene smiled and jumped out of bed in nothing but her underwear. As Shadow made his way to her open window, Darlene passed her hand down the fur of his back. He ignored her as he usually did and was soon gone. Darlene smirked and went into her closet to get dressed for the day.

Chapter 26 – Patrick Web

The boy's name was Patrick Web. He was seventeen and shared a number of classes with Darlene. He was tall and clean-cut. His eyes were piercing blue, and he had an interesting talent for making people look away when he looked at them. It was a skill in which he was quite proud of.

As far as his studies, Patrick always found a way. He was not particularly smart, but he always seemed to have a near magical influence over those around him. Some said it was because he was wealthy; others said it was pure charm. Whatever the case, he always got his way.

Patrick had three friends who always seemed to follow in his shadow. They were Billy, Rich, and Tucker. Their story was not of as much consequence as they were simply there for Patrick. It was a friendship of convenience built around the one boy who seemed to have some sort of power over the world around them, and if they could only remain at his side, perhaps, they could have some of this power as well.

It was the end of another school day. Patrick had not really been paying attention in any of his classes, and he had skipped one of them. Although, he had been given a talking to by the principal for doing it, that was the whole of his consequences. This had been par for the course. Presently, the group of four boys were hanging around Patrick's locker.

"Whoa, have you seen Darlene lately, Pat?" asked Billy looking around nervously.

"You mean Little Red?" asked Patrick with a smirk. The other boys chuckled. "An't my type," he added.

Rich remarked, "You an't seen her out of the jacket yet."

"Who told you that?" asked the leader of the group.

"Just sayin'," said Rich a bit more meekly.

"She isn't my type," repeated Patrick. "She's bookish. She skips grades like we skip classes."

Tucker then said, "But she don't really look the part. I mean... Have you looked in those eyes? She's got a secret a bet."

Patrick did not respond; however, he understood what Tucker was talking about. There *was* something odd about the girl. He had tried to avoid her because he was not interested in the nerdy type of girls, but there had always been something distinctly *not-nerdy* about her. He was not sure what it was.

Rich got enough courage to ask, "You ever wonder why she dresses like that?"

Billy agreed, "Yeah, like she's in a storybook." He whispered, "Sounds kind of kinky to me." They all turned to hide their faces as they snickered.

Patrick shook his head. "I gotta admit, the Little Red bit is weird. She's gotta be doing it on purpose. She kind of make it work too."

Tucker asked, "Soooo... do you like her?"

Patrick whispered, "Only if I get to be the wolf."

Darlene stepped out of a classroom causing the boys to straighten up. She was wearing a jacket with a red hood with a string that was tied around her neck. She saw that the boys were staring at her and stopped to see what it was all about. "Something wrong?" she asked them.

"Oh, no, no! We're just fine," said Patrick brushing off the guys around him. "We've just been joking around."

She stared at Patrick for a short time. Their eyes met in those moments, and something snapped within the boy. He saw something in her that he could not explain. Suddenly, he was no longer just curious in the girl; he was interested.

"Okay then," said Darlene as she gracefully turned to walk away.

"Hey, wait!" called Patrick. Without thinking, he reached out and snatched the girl's arm bringing her to a halt.

Darlene found herself looking into his eyes again. She was silent and submissive as he gazed at her. Patrick boldly said to Darlene, "Mind if I call you Little Red?"

Billy, Rich, and Tucker burst out laughing. They had assumed that he had just made a joke to hurt the girl. It was in his nature and he had done so before. Oddly, Darlene barely reacted to the question. She looked down at the hand holding onto her arm and then back at him. She asked, "Is that what you want?"

"That's what I want," he replied. The other boys were starting to get the idea that it had not been a joke. They rather awkwardly sidled away from the two; although, they still watched from a distance.

Darlene smiled for a moment. She removed his hand from his arm and asked, "What does that make you?"

Patrick chuckled and answered, "Well, I an't your grandma."

The girl shook her head. "Sorry, I'm not playing this game with you."

She started to walk away, but he persisted, "Come on, Little Red, hear me out. I just wanna be friends. I'm not all bad like everyone makes me out to be. I'm just messin' with ya."

"Whatever," she said.

She had made it ten paces away from him before he called to her, "What are you so afraid of?!"

She stopped. Taking a deep breath, she turned around and walked back to him. Glaring into his strong eyes, she said, "I'm not afraid of anything–especially not the Big Bad Wolf."

Patrick shrugged. "Well, you would know, Little Red. But if you an't afraid of nothin', perhaps, you'd like to join me for a little party this weekend at my place. My parents won't be there... but if you're afraid, I understand."

Darlene smiled, and it completely surprised him. Slowly, she reached up her hand and touched the confused boy's nose. "All right," she cooed. And then she simply turned and walked away. Patrick stood stock-still as she left the building entirely. His gang were all around him in the next moment talking about how cool the scene had been to them, but he barely heard them. At that moment, his only thoughts were about her... and what he wanted to do to her.

Chapter 27 – The Scent

That night, Darlene was in her room gazing idly at her favorite book. She was looking more at the pictures than really reading it. The girl could recite the story by heart and even act it out physically if she desired to. Presently, she was only looking at it.

There was a noise just outside her window, and she turned her head just in time to see the large wolf with yellow eyes leap up into the room. "Hey, Shadow," said Darlene looking back at her book.

"Yeah," said the wolf jumping up into her bed.

Darlene did not always talk to Shadow. Many of his visits were just so they could be together, but tonight, he walked up to her and bumped the back of her book. Suddenly, there was a large wolf snout in her face. "What's the matter with you?" she asked.

"Your scent," he said tersely. "Who have you been with?"

"Who?" she asked just a little nervously. "I was at school. I was around a lot of people."

Shadow snorted and growled at her briefly. "I am being lied to."

"About being around lots of people at school? How is that a lie?"

He scowled. "I am no fool, Darlene. I can smell him all over you." He pushed his snout towards her again taking another whiff. "Your arm is where it is the strongest; however, the stench is all over you."

Darlene giggled. "Since when do you care when I bump into people?!"

"You are a liar!" he snapped.

The girl pushed the wolf's head away. "It's just school! Leave me alone!"

Shadow stumbled only slightly but was soon on top of her with his claws to her chest. "Who is he?" he growled.

Darlene took deep breaths as she looked into his eyes. She was not entirely upset with how Shadow was treating her. In fact, she was actually rather excited by it. After a few moments, she smiled. Shadow pounded on her chest once with his paws and then walked to the other side of the bed growling.

The strike had knocked her breath away a little bit. The girl coughed but still smiled. "You're worried over nothing. I still belong to you, don't I?"

The sullen wolf grumbled. "Indeed, but you can still be stolen from me. I have not waited all these years for nothing. I also detest your insincerity to me. You have forgotten the nature of our relationship."

She bumped his hide with her foot from under the comforter. "That was ages ago, Shadow. We're closer than we've ever been. Don't try and make this out to be something that it isn't."

"You are a stupid girl if you believe anything of what you have just said. Humans change; I do not."

She picked her book back up and said, "Whatever. I still love you."

The wolf did not reply. He simply lay where he was for a time before asking, "Who is he?"

She slammed the book down on her lap. "What does it matter?!"

He snarled. "The scent of his lust looms even now around my head! Tell me who he is!"

"No!" she said behind nervous laughter. "I'm sixteen. I can have a life outside the one I have with you."

"You won't be alive for much longer," he muttered.

"Whatever," she said again.

He looked at her and said, "You will tell me who it is before morning. I'll keep you up all night if you don't."

"Don't care," she swiftly replied raising the book back up.

He stood back up and faced her. "Are you amused by all this?"

"Totally," she said from behind her book.

He swatted the book from her hands and snapped at her face. Darlene scowled and boldly pushed him off of her bed. He tried to get back up, but she pushed him off a second time. Shadow slowly walked around the bed to the other side. The girl tossed her covers away and began crawling on her hands and knees in only her panties. "Go on! Try again!" she goaded him.

Shadow faked to the right and managed to get up on the bed. She laughed and leapt at him wrapping her arms around his neck. She managed to wrestle him onto his side, but he was widely kicking and scratching trying to get back up. Darlene struggled to hold him, but they both ended up slipping off the edge of the bed onto the floor.

A little stunned by the fall, Darlene was suddenly pounced by a very angry wolf. "Who is he?!" he shouted.

"You gonna eat me or what?!" she challenged him.

"Yes!" he snapped. "I'm going to tear you to bits! Now, tell me who he is!"

"You're full of it, Shadow! You're not gonna kill anyone! You can't even kill me! Now, get off of me!" She put all her weight into rolling him off of her. When he tried to pounce her again, Darlene pulled the comforter off of the bed draping it over him. While he was disoriented, she jumped back on the bed with a smile.

It took him a moment, but he was soon able to get from under the quilt. He shot the girl a scowl as he slowly walked back towards the window. "He will *not* have you," he said like it was a promise.

Darlene dropped down to her belly. She kicked up her bare feet and cooed out the words, "Leaving so soon?"

"Your days are numbered. Enjoy every moment of life you have."

"Whatever," she said again.

Before he left, Shadow added, "And be sure that I shall be the only one to devour you."

"Love you, Shadow," she cooed, but he was already gone.

Chapter 28 – Through the Window

It was Saturday night. Darlene was in her room putting on her red jacket when there was a sudden knock at her door. "Darlene?" came the voice of her mother.

The girl scowled and quickly tossed her jacket into the closet. "What is it, mom?"

"Can I see you for a little bit?"

"I was just going to bed," said Darlene tossing on a pink bathrobe to cover up her clothing. She then went to the door and unlocked it. "Come on in."

Samantha opened up to see her sixteen-year-old daughter yawning. "It's a bit early, isn't it?" asked the mother.

Darlene backed away and went for her bed. "I'm just really tired tonight. Did you need me for anything?" She sat on her bed and tried to look as sleepy as she could.

Samantha closed the door once she had come in. She sat next to her daughter in silence. The action confused the girl. "What's the matter?" asked Darlene.

Samantha replied, "Is everything okay, honey?"

"What do you mean? I'm just tired today. I had all this homework today, and you know how hard I try to get good grades, mom."

"Yes, I know," nodded the mother. "I just mean in general. Is there anything in your life you feel I should know about?"

Darlene was a little blindsided by the question. "Like what? What's bringing this on? Is everything okay with *you*?"

Samantha placed a hand to her daughter's back. "It just seems like… something's been on your mind lately. You know I really do love you, right?" The words came from lips which trembled ever so slightly. It was almost as if Samantha was frightened about something she did not understand.

Darlene looked at the floor for a little bit before replying, "It's just school, mom. I'm worried I won't pass this big math test that's coming up. The teacher has been *really* strict with everybody, and it's totally unfair."

Samantha's expression seemed unchanged. Had she believed what she was told? It was confusing to Darlene. It was usually pretty easy to get rid of her mother. Samantha finally said, "I'm sure you'll do fine as long as you work really hard on it." The backrub turned into an embrace. "Are you sure that's all that's bothering you?"

Darlene was suddenly uncomfortable. "Mom, I'm fine. I just wanna sleep tonight. Is that all right with you?"

Samantha sighed deeply and then nodded. "It's fine with me, honey. I'm sorry if I seem so worried. I just love you very much."

"I know. I love you too, mom." They hugged, and then Samantha walked back to the door. After taking one more look at her daughter, she pulled it shut.

Darlene waited for half a minute before getting out of bed, turning off the lights, and relocking the door. She then quickly discarded the bathrobe and threw on her red jacket. Quietly, she pushed open her window and jumped out into the bushes that were planted just outside. It was a calm night; although, she heard there might be rain later.

After taking a few steps into the side yard, she heard the growling voice of a certain wolf, "She is beginning to sense me."

Darlene stopped with a roll of her eyes. She turned to see Shadow walking out of the bushes as well. He was barely visible in this area because there was very little light between the two houses. She asked, "*Who* is?"

"Your mother," he replied slowly walking around the girl. "It has taken her nearly your entire life, but she is now just starting to get it."

"Well, she won't," said Darlene. "And neither will dad."

Shadow snorted. "Your father doesn't want to see me. He gave up on seeing me many years ago. He is a stupid fool and entirely a failure as a father."

Darlene was more annoyed that Shadow had found her sneaking away at all. She addressed the issue by asking, "You aren't going to follow me around all night, are you?"

The wolf lashed her legs with his tail as he walked around her. "You think this is all a game. You actually think that you have control over your own existence in this world… and also me."

"Whatever makes you feel better, Shadow," she said defiantly.

Shadow suddenly snaked his body through her legs which nearly knocked her over. She tried to kick him, but it was as if he was able to fade into the shadows of the yard for just that moment. When she was able to see him clearly again, he said, "You have absolutely no idea how close you are to being devoured by me. The minutes of your life are ticking away to that precise moment where you will say those precious words I have wanted you to say since the day we first met."

"What words?" she asked with a scowl.

Ignoring her question, he continued, "And when I hear those delicious words come forth from your lips, I shall sink my teeth into your neck and *rrrrip* it out!"

"You could have done that ages ago," she accused him.

The wolf sat upon his haunches in front of her bedroom window and cocked his head. "You have no inkling at all of what is at stake. You simply think you shall die and then all your pain will end in a quick moment. Darlene, you shall be consumed for eternity, and that shall be your death. It shall be a never-ending and irreconcilable issue for you, but for me, it shall be quite delicious."

The girl huffed as if she had heard him talk like that many times before, and now, it had simply become boring to her. "Are you finished?"

"I shall be quite soon, Darlene." Saying those words, he walked into the bushes and disappeared from her vision altogether. The girl looked around for him a few times before running off into the darkness to meet with Patrick Web.

Chapter 29 – "Little Red"

Patrick only lived a couple miles away from Darlene, but the location was a very different one. It was a large house on the edge of a cliff side. It had a big garage in front and a pool in the back. Darlene was impressed. The whole place made her feel simple.

The first thing that seemed a little strange to the girl was the lack of noise. She expected to hear a lot of music and yelling at the place. The only sounds she could hear were crickets, the wind, and the distant sounds of thunder. For a moment, she wondered if she had come to the wrong place.

Darlene rang the doorbell and knocked. Nothing. She looked through the window to see if she could see anyone. There was a darkened foyer and a staircase visible, but otherwise, it was devoid of any life. Darlene leaned against the door with her arms crossed and grumbled, "Complete waste of time."

A voice seemed to come from an unknown direction, "Little Red!"

Darlene looked around and was soon smiling. She left the front door and began to look about the area. It was not very well lit. There was a high lamppost set up in the driveway which helped a little, but she still could not see anyone.

"Hey, Little Red!" came the voice again.

Darlene turned about and began walking around the house towards the back. She had glimpsed the pool slightly as she was coming through the woods. She wondered why she did not even consider going back there first. Perhaps, it was all the quiet. The backside of the house was much better lit, but there was still no sign of life. With a huff, Darlene began walking towards the cliff just to see the view.

Although it was dark, there was still much to see. There was another city down below, and there were lights sprinkled about the bottom as if the stars were below her. She could also see silent flashes of light coming from the horizon followed by the distant rumbling of thunder. Darlene hoped the storm was not coming her way. She wanted to enjoy herself.

Suddenly, Darlene felt a hand upon both of her shoulders. "Little Red," said Patrick into her ear.

The girl gasped out but did not scream. She became rigid for a moment before turning around to look into his eyes. "You lied to me," she said to him.

He gestured towards himself. "I… I lied to you? When have I ever lied to you, my dear Little Red?"

"You said you were having a party tonight," she explained.

"It *is* a party. We're together. We're a party of two."

"Two?" she repeated unconvinced.

"That's right," Patrick replied with a smile. "Little red… and the Big Bad Wolf. That's what you wanted, right?"

The way he had said the latter was rife with a certain threatening lust. It was clear rather than subtle. It opened Darlene's eyes to her situation, and she was not afraid. In fact, the girl smiled and began to walk slowly around Patrick in a very teasing way. "I guess I should be frightened," she cooed.

There was no question that the boy really, *really* liked what she was doing. It was entirely not what he had expected. In truth, Patrick was prepared for a struggle. He had been in that situation before. Little girls like this were easy enough to deal with, but Little Red was playing the victim. She *wanted* it. Although it was driving him wild, it was also holding him back. He wanted to see how far she would go.

"You like the wolves, don't you, Little Red?" he said with a smirk.

She circled him again and ran a finger over the boy's nose. He tried to nip at it, but she pulled it away. "Why would you say that?" she asked playfully. "They're always trying to eat me up."

"I can see why," he said with a half-chuckle.

"But no matter what happens," she went on to say. "No matter how hard he tries, the Big Bad Wolf never gets me."

"Gonna have to take care of that," said Patrick under his breath.

The thunder was not quite as distant as it had been. It was closer now and little droplets of water fell here and there. Neither boy nor girl seemed to care. It was all about the two of them. She was circling, and he was letting her.

He was enjoying it, but he knew it could only go on for so long.

Darlene stopped in front of him. Slowly, she pulled down her red hood and undid her jacket letting it slip from her body to the ground. The girl then laid her hand upon his nose and asked, "Who's afraid of the Big Bad Wolf?"

Patrick chuckled. He pushed her hand away from his face and cleared his throat. "So, eh, you gonna take your clothes off or am I gonna have to do it?"

The statement confused Darlene. "You're supposed to play along."

The boy shook his head. "Look, I gotta say. That was freaking hot what you did there, but this wolf is ready to eat you the hell up. So, one more time: you gonna strip or am I gonna do it for you?"

She glared at him for a moment before turning away. He grabbed her arm and yanked her back saying, "Looks like it's gonna be the wolf."

"Stop it!" she screamed as he forced his hand into the neck of her shirt ripping it apart with amazing strength. She struggled and cried out, but he only laughed and struck her to keep her in line. Finally, when the sixteen-year-old girl was topless, he tossed her to the ground just as the rain began to come down more rapidly upon them both.

Darlene was crying. The whole thing had been a surprise to her. She never thought he would have done that. Patrick took a moment to look at the wet girl laying before him in the grass. He had been here before, but this was not just any girl–this was Little Red. This was his own personal little fantasy he had had since he ran into her at school. He was going to enjoy this more than any other time.

His train of thought was broken by the sounds of growling. There was a flash of light which revealed a large beast slowly coming towards him from the trees that surrounded the house. "Whoa!" Patrick shouted backing away into the light of the backyard. Darlene grabbed her torn clothing and ran away.

The yellow-eyed beast was baring its teeth. Saliva was dripping in copious amounts from his jaws as it snarled with rage. "Hey, get back, Fido!" yelled Patrick.

There was an old rusted pipe laying near the pool that had been left there after some recent maintenance. He picked it up and swung at the creature a few times. "Get back! I'll bash your head in, you mutt!"

The wolf stopped when it was swung at, but it did not seemed threatened by it at all. Instead of running away from Patrick, the creature opened its snarling muzzle and growled out the words, "She… is… *mine!*"

Hearing the creature talk was enough to confuse the boy into a stupor. There was a distinct moment where he was not entirely sure what he was looking at; however, he never had time to figure it out. The beast took the opening to leap upon him. Patrick was forced to the ground and his throat was very quickly ripped out. His blood flowed forth onto the ground running free with the rain water that was everywhere around him. Darlene had only been standing a short distance away. She had seen everything.

Shadow looked at her as he stood over the twitching, gurgling boy. Darlene was the picture of fear as she stood there soaking wet and still trying to keep herself covered. Another flash of lightning and rumble of thunder passed over their heads. The wolf said to her, "Go back to your room, Darlene. I shall be dealing with you shortly."

The girl backed away from Shadow. The wolf had begun tearing the boy up right in front of her. He was feeding off of him. It was a terrible thing to see. She had thought about it countless times, but this was the first time she had seen it. The girl turned and ran as fast as she could back to her house. The rain hid her tears.

Chapter 30 – The Storm

Darlene sat up in her bed with her arms wrapped around her folded legs. She was still very wet from running through the storm. Her eyes stared ahead as if looking at something horrible, but there was nothing else in the room but her. The truth was that she had finally come to realize exactly where she stood in the world, and it was not a good thing at all.

The window made a sound. Darlene saw it open on its own. There was only light visibility presently. The storm outside was a powerful one, and lightening was frequent. She briefly caught a glimpse of the form of a wolf leaping into the room. Darlene watched for the creature carefully.

The bed wobbled and she soon saw his yellow eyes staring across into hers. In a whimper, Darlene asked, "Why did you kill him?"

Shadow replied, "He was going to devour you."

"No. He was… he wasn't going to… devour me."

"I saw it in his eyes," said the creature. "I would not let him. That shall be my pleasure, Darlene… tonight."

"When tonight?" she asked.

"When you say what I wish to hear."

*****

Samantha jumped as a sudden clash of thunder roared over the house. She was in bed with Lucas who had been reading a novel. He put his arm around her and asked, "You okay, dear? You've been jumpy all evening."

171

The mother looked at him and said, "I don't know. It just feels like... I don't know... like something's wrong."

"Not afraid of the storm, are you?" he asked with a chuckle.

Samantha looked in the direction of Darlene's room. "I'm not sure."

He smiled and continued to rub her back. "It reminds me back when Darlene was eight-months-old. She was crying, and you were desperate to go out and comfort her."

"She needed me," said the mother with a slight whimper.

"Who knows why babies cry?" said Lucas. "The point was that we needed Darlene to be independent. They shouldn't always rely on us to take care of everything."

Samantha looked at him. "But what if some things are too big for one person to handle alone? Darlene's a strong girl, I know, but she's only human."

"We did the best we could," assured the father. "You don't have to worry about Darlene."

Samantha stared straight ahead and worried regardless. She could not help but worry. Something was wrong. Something had always been wrong. It was like she was just realizing that something horrible was right in the house with her and that it had always been there... just hiding somewhere in the shadows. A clever something that reveled in the fact that she never could see it. The only problem was that the mother had no idea what it could possibly be.

Another thunder clashed, and Samantha jumped once more. Lucas suggested, "Maybe, you could use some warm milk or something."

"Yes," she said after a quick moment of thought. "I'll go get some warm milk." She tossed aside her covers and got out of bed. "I'll be right back."

"Sure," said Lucas looking back at his book.

Samantha walked through the house as the thunder and lightning continued outside fiercer than ever. The lights in the house flickered for a moment giving the woman pause. It felt wrong. It all felt wrong. It was in the very air she was breathing–like the air itself was electric. It was a stifling atmosphere.

She felt it the most as she was passing Darlene's room. The mother stopped where she was and just stared at the door. Darlene had gone to sleep so early that night. Was she all right? Did she need help? Samantha had never felt so helpless before in all of her life. It was not so much a feeling that she could not do anything, but only that there was something horrible simply to be found on the other side of that door.

Quietly–as not to wake her–Samantha tried the doorknob. It was locked as usual. She released the knob and contemplated going back to Lucas. She took a few steps in that very direction but stopped herself once more. The door had a simple lock on it. Any small screwdriver could turn the mechanism inside. Samantha went into the kitchen and retrieved the tool from a drawer before returning.

The mother carefully inserted the screwdriver into the opening and ever so carefully turned. There was a *click*. This sound caused Samantha such pangs of anxiety that she immediately tossed away the tool and threw open the door.

A substantial flash of lightning illuminated Darlene's room for nearly two seconds. Darlene was sitting in her bed with a very large wolf who had just turned its yellow eyes to look at the intruder. The mother screamed, and the beast fled out of the open window into the raging storm. "Darlene!" cried Samantha.

Darlene jumped out of bed and screamed, "Get out of here, mom!"

"What was that?!" said Samantha near hysterical. She wondered why Lucas had not heard her.

Darlene marched up to her mother with tears in her eyes. "It was Shadow, okay?! You remember him? That wolf that never existed?! Now, get out!"

Samantha broke out into tears as she tried to take hold of her struggling daughter's shoulders. "What… What is happening, Darlene?! I don't understand! I love you! You have to tell me everything!"

The words seemed to touch the girl for a moment, but she soon broke down and sobbed, "What's the point?! You never listened to me! I was always trying to tell you!"

"Tell me what?!" cried the mother.

"Shadow is real!" Darlene cried just as lightning struck just outside of the window. The noise had been deafening. "He's going to kill me, and there's nothing I can do to stop him. So just leave me alone! You never bothered to care about me anyways!"

Samantha took the girls face in her trembling hands. "But I *do* love you! I want to help you! I need you to believe me, Darlene!"

"Too late!" cried Darlene before slapping her mother aside. She pushed past Samantha and ran for the front door.

"Darlene!" cried Samantha hysterically as she ran after her daughter.

The girl swiped her mother's purse from the foyer table and threw open the front door. She ran out into the storm without looking back. Samantha ran out into the front yard only to see her daughter fade into the shadows of the storm. She tripped and fell into a puddle that had formed in the front yard. "Darlene, please dome back! Darlene!"

Meanwhile, Lucas was still in his room reading a book. He had not heard a thing. He did not suspect a thing. He had no idea that his daughter was gone.

Chapter 31 – Scarlett and the Wolf

"Welcome back," said the host as the audience applauded. "We will be continuing our on campus interview with the esteemed Doctor Thaddeus Rule. I'm your host Frederick Pence. Welcome back, Doctor Rule."

"Thank you," said the doctor with a smile. They were both sitting in chairs upon a stage surrounded by college students. A book was on display between them.

Mister Pence continued, "If you're just joining us, we were discussing the distinguished career of Doctor Rule. He is widely believed to be the best in the world when it comes to child psychology. He has had patients across the globe with some of the most remarkable stories included in those cases. He is also an author, aren't you, Doctor Rule?"

"Yes, I have penned a few books in my day," chuckled Rule.

"But the one we all *really* want to talk about this evening is your most recent book which is aptly entitled *Scarlett and the Wolf.*" The host picked up the book off of the table and showed it to the audience. "I must say, this may be one of the most peculiar cases in psychology I have ever read about. It almost seems a work of fiction."

"Oh, it's true," said Doctor Rule. "Scarlett was a real little girl who had formed a dangerous bond with an imaginary wolf who quite hated her."

"Yes," said Mister Pence with a chuckle. "It's hard to believe that this actually happened. It was quite a journey for you too, it seems. You spent a good amount of time trying to gain her trust. What was that like?"

Rule explained, "It wasn't easy, I admit. Scarlett was absolutely positive that this creature known as Shadow existed. She was very protective of this fact, and I learned that much of it was from a delusion that the creature was very real. To complicate matters, her mother gave her a very strangely edited copy of *Little Red Riding-Hood* that perpetuated her mania in very unhealthy ways."

"Yes, tell us more about that book. It was very interesting."

Doctor Rule chuckled and pressed a finger to his chin. "Yes, the book. There is a strange version of the story written by seventeenth century author Charles Perrault whose interpretation of the story seemed to portray a subtle sexual relationship between girl and wolf. The version Scarlett's mother gave her was slightly edited to have a peculiar repetition of the wolf's name written as... Master Wolf. Although throughout the story, this happened mainly within the scene where the two are doing their famous Q and A–all the bigger to see you with and that sort of business.

"This particular version of the story can be misinterpreted to show Little Red as being the instigator of the whole thing. She agrees with the wolf to race to Grandmother's house and conveniently forgets about the wolf when she arrives. She appears to know that it is the wolf that is in bed instead of her grandmother but chooses not to say anything about it. And when the wolf invites her into bed with him, she disrobes and enters into the bed with the naked wolf. She is then eaten alive shortly after at which point the story ends abruptly."

"No hunter?" asked the host.

"No, the hunter came about in the Grimm tales. Scarlett interpreted the Perrault version of the story literally and formed a submissive bond with Shadow who–might I also point out–was very adamant about wanting to devour her. It even seemed that she *wanted* him to eat her–as disturbing as that sounds. Either way, she wasn't dealing with reality. She was quite literally giving herself to *Master Wolf* in the form of Shadow the imaginary wolf."

Mister Pence replied, "Fascinating. Now, in the chapter you entitled 'Believing in Shadow,' you explained that, for a time, you had to force yourself to actually accept the imaginary as reality as a way to identify with Scarlett's mania."

Rule rolled his eyes for a moment. "That was a journey unto itself."

"I imagine it would be," said the host. "You had to trick yourself into believing in the unreal. It sounds as if you allowed yourself to go mad."

"It was controlled, but yes. I wanted to become this girl's friend. Her parents had already turned against Shadow which had caused the girl to act out in a violent way. To prevent a return of that event, it was important for me to believe her entirely."

The host added, "And in doing so, you formed quite a fantastic opinion of Shadow in the process."

Doctor Rule leaned back into his chair and nodded. "I learned who he was."

"What do you mean by that exactly?"

"No one understood Shadow more than Scarlett did, but I was a better judge of character. The more I listened to her talk about this creature, the more I started to see him myself. I was able to form an entire picture in my mind about him–enough to put down succinctly into words. I'm not surprised you're bringing this up. It's been the most controversial part of the whole book."

"I can see why," said Mister Pence. "You expound for many pages about a fictional character as if he was a real entity."

"I was venting, I suppose. A product of my madness, as you called it. I really began to understand this creature far more than Scarlett did. He became real to *me*. He was my enemy, and I needed to know what I was fighting against. I chose to deliver it to the reader in a very direct way… which may have been folly; however, I stand by my decision."

The host nodded and asked, "Can you explain your impressions of this imaginary wolf for our audience."

Doctor Rule seemed momentarily uncomfortable; however, he ultimately nodded his head and said, "I would be happy to. With Shadow the wolf, we have more than a simple creature being given the gift of speech. He was far too conniving for that. I felt a certain cleverness there that seemed to be working against me. I was never his friend, and he was never mine. He was neither the friend of Scarlett; however, he was clearly her possessor. He did so with a pride that came with centuries of accomplishment. He was a villain undefeated even in ancient times.

"It is distinctly possible that this creature may have at one time taken on a more human-like existence, as some illustrations portray the frightening Master Wolf, but such things are not acceptable in modern days. He travels about the world like a common beast and seeks out prey until he finds something that really interests him. At that moment, all the devious motives of his past life come flooding back, and he becomes reminiscent of those years where he could sully the beauty of human youth with such flare.

"It is not only a fact that Shadow is ancient and likely immortal, it is entirely possible that he provides the basis for all wolf villains throughout history which goes back even into the early days of Greece and their *Aesop's Fables*. He has powers that are supernatural–one of which suppresses the wills of those whom he considers weak minded. If a man or woman does not directly go against him, he can darken their minds so that he becomes invisible to them. This latter point would explain why the parents never heard or saw Shadow for all those years. They never saw him because they did not want to see him, and in the same way, Shadow had taken control of their wills and dominated their spirits. I would even go so far as to say that Shadow could blatantly turn Scarlett's parents into his own obedient thralls if enough will could be sapped from them.

"His domination of Scarlett was likely caused by some sort of act of defiance on behalf of the girl. He was going to gobble her up; however, he was stayed by an act that he did not expect–in this case, a touch to his nose. It did not stop him from wanting to eat her, but merely encouraged him not to do the act by halves. He would bring

181

her up to an appropriate age where he could remove the aspect of her that opposed him and then do away with her at the time of his preference. He would still feed off lesser beings until then; however, the act of killing Scarlett would be a spiritually significant one such as destroying the potential of a soul at a crucial moment. It very likely could make him far more powerful than he was prior–not to mention his renewed spirit for his ancient cause."

Doctor Rule suddenly stopped talking. He pressed his head to his hand and groaned a bit. The host asked, "Are you all right, Doctor Rule?"

"Oh yes. Just a head ache. I suppose it is not an easy thing to elaborate on madness–especially my own. Of course, it's all rubbish. Scarlett was only under the oppression of her own active imagination. But ah!" He grabbed his head again and the lights of the room flickered for just a moment. The doctor looked into a dark place between the two rows of students, and it seemed on his face as if he saw something frightening.

"Sorry about that," said Mister Pence. "That's the problem with live broadcasts. There's a storm just outside, and we lost power to some of our lights for a moment. But Doctor, I really am impressed by your insight not only into Scarlett but also into her own terrible creation."

Doctor Rule looked at the host as if he had seen a ghost. He said, "Did you see that? I think it was grinning at me."

Pence just looked at him for a moment before turning to the camera. "And that's all the time we have for tonight. Be sure to pick up a copy of *Scarlett and the Wolf*. I guarantee you won't regret it. One of the most fascinating case studies out there. Thank you, Doctor Thaddeus Rule, and I'm your host, Fredrick Pence, wishing you all a good night."

Before the show closed out, Doctor Rule was seen ripping the microphone from his tie and walking off of the stage. He looked ill. The host simply stayed where he was and watched him leave.

Chapter 32 – The Words

Mister Finch could not believe how bad the weather had gotten. It had entirely defied the reports on TV. There was now a major curfew in effect for the entire county, and nobody seemed to understand what it really was that was happening in the sky.

Finch jumped a little as his windows began rattling. They had never done that before. The winds outside were blowing so hard. He sniffed and tried to relax again. Certainly, there would be nobody out there tonight needing a room. The Motor Inn would have a lot of vacancies that night.

The man turned on some music and tried to calm down. He had been through storms before. He had no idea why he was so antsy. It felt like something was just off. He had never felt like something was this far off before. Of course, it was just his imagination. He kept telling himself that because it had to be true. He would just have to get used to those rattling windows one way or another. He reached over and picked up a mug of chocolate.

There was a sudden beating upon the lobby door. Mister Finch was suddenly covered in chocolate. He cursed and wiped himself off as he walked over to the door. "I'm coming!" he shouted.

He took a peek out of a nearby window and was surprised to see it was a teenage girl who was soaking wet. He quickly unlocked the door and threw it open. Rain blasted into the room past the girl. "Good lord! Where did you come from?!" he shouted trying to pull her inside.

The girl was crying and holding a purse. She wasted no time in pulling out a wad of bills and holding it up to the man. "I need a room right now."

"You're a mess," he said. "Are you in trouble? I can call the police."

"Just take my money and give me a room!" She shoved the bills into his hand.

Mister Finch looked at the money. It was more than enough, but the situation was far from common. "I'll not do anything unless you explain to me what you were doing out there in the middle of… that nightmare out there. Where are your parents?"

"It's not gonna matter!" she nearly screamed. "They can't help me!"

"Well, that may be so, but I really think you should at least give me a way to contact them."

The girl dug around in the purse and took out a pen and an old receipt. She went to the counter and wrote down a number. "This is my parent's number. Can I have my key now?"

Mister Finch looked at it for a moment as he took down a key from the wall. "You're in room 101. You want me to take you there?"

She swiped the key. "No! I just want you to leave me alone!" She ran back out into the rain slamming the door behind her.

Mister Finch looked out of a window to make sure she made it into her room. When he was satisfied, he walked over to his desk to make the phone call. When he held the number up to look at it, the lights flickered and went out. "Damn it," he groaned. "Perfect timing."

"Precisely," came a deep voice from somewhere. The innkeeper looked around and saw two yellow eyes in the darkness. A moment later, he was on the floor feeling his throat being ripped out.

*****

Darlene sat on the bed of the motel room and stared forward as if in a trance. Nothing about the room was nice. It was a subpar establishment at best. Something about this fact seemed to make her situation all the more poignant. Darlene could actually see the end of her life as a light that was about to be switched off for eternity. It was a very real and vivid sensation. Her life was nearly over, and it was only minutes away.

The lights in the room flickered. Several of the bulbs popped leaving only one of them on. Darlene looked around at the floor trying to spot the wolf. He was not there. She felt alone. She felt entirely alone. Or was she?

She looked to her left and there was Shadow's two cold eyes and grinning maw right next to her. "Hello, Darlene."

"Oh, God," she said in a trembling voice.

"This is a very special night... for *me*," said Shadow. He slowly walked around to her front. "I've waited a very long time for this. How are you feeling, Darlene?"

The girl shook her head. "I don't want it. I've changed my mind."

187

Shadow chuckled as he slowly began to crawl over the girl's front. "I want you to say the words."

Darlene broke out in a fit of crying. "I don't know what you wanna hear, Shadow. Why are you doing this to me?"

As he crawled up the girl's soaked body, she was compelled to lay down flat. His front paws seemed to grab the pillow around her head as if they were a pair of clawed hands. In a snarling voice, he ordered her, "Say… the words, Darlene."

She continued to tremble underneath his large form. Shadow seemed much bigger somehow. He was pressed hard against her, and she did not think that she could overpower him. Darlene whimpered out, "I don't want to die, Shadow!"

The wolf chuckled deeply. "Oh, that is *so* close to what I want to hear." He ripped one side of her pillow to shreds suddenly before putting his claws back there. She screamed when he did this. He added, "I can smell the blood flowing inside you. I can even see it. Your heart beats still. It gives you warmth and life. I wonder how much it weighs, Darlene. I think I should like to have a look at it."

"Please, stop it, Shadow! I love you!"

"Say the words!" he snapped.

Darlene broke out into a hysterical fit of crying. Shadow remained very close to her face pressing himself against her. She looked into his yellow eyes and was, at once, compelled to say what he wanted to hear. In a pathetic whimper, Darlene spoke, "I'm afraid."

Shadow began to laugh. Thunder and lightning blasted across the outside sky so hard that the ground began to quake. "Say it again!" he cried out with vicious jubilation.

"I'm really afraid! Please, don't kill me, Shadow! I love you!"

Once more, the wolf laughed and reveled in the beautiful words that he had waited so long to hear from this girl. The joy soon turned into a snarl, and his eyes became firmly set upon the girl as if she was nothing to him at all.

"Shadow," she whimpered.

He growled. He snarled. He slobbered and spit. His teeth were bared with lips curled up and trembling with hatred. His eyes pierced into her soul with rage. The windows of the room began to rattle and crack. The bed was trembling under a powerful ethereal force.

Terrified, Darlene slowly lifted up her trembling hand towards the wolf's nose. "Please, don't," she whimpered. "Please." She was almost able to touch him, but Shadow suddenly shot his toothy maw forward directly into Darlene's neck.

Bibliography

In the course of writing this book, I slightly edited a copy of *Little Red Riding-Hood* as written by Charles Perrault. The copy I used as a basis for my version of the story was found in the book cited below:

Perrault, Charles, 1628-1703. <u>The Complete Fairy Tales / Charles Perrault</u>. New York: Oxford University Press, 2009. Kindle Edition.